# ⭐#1 SPACE CADETS

## Jerks-in-Training

### R.L. Stine

AN
**APPLE**
PAPERBACK

SCHOLASTIC INC.
New York Toronto London Auckland Sydney

ISBN 0-590-44745-9

12 11 10 9 8 7 6 5 4 3 2 1          1 2 3 4 5 6/9

Printed in the U.S.A          28

First Scholastic printing, August 1991

# Jerks-in-Training

# 1

Cadet Beef Hardy walked smartly down the corridor, the heels of his perfectly polished boots clicking rhythmically on the marble floor. His gold and gray cadet uniform was pressed and spotless, the brass buttons shined to a golden glow.

As he strode purposefully toward the Commander's office, he swung his right hand at a 40-degree arc. The regulation cadet arm swing.

One of the new cadet plebes approached, a timid-looking young man named Fenster. Cadet Hardy stopped to acknowledge Fenster's salute. Then his right fist shot out like a lightning bolt, catching the surprised plebe hard on the nose.

Stunned, Fenster staggered backward, grabbing his nose. "Why'd you do that, sir?" he asked.

"Just testing my hand speed, plebe," Hardy sneered. "You don't mind if I test my reflexes on your face, do you?"

"Uh . . . no, sir," the frightened plebe said meekly.

"You're bleeding on the floor," Hardy said, pointing a perfectly manicured, accusing finger. "That's against regulations, Fenster. Violation 256–B. Put yourself on report."

"Yes, sir," Fenster said, saluting with one hand, cupping his ruined nose with the other, and hurrying off miserably down the hall to report himself for disciplinary action.

Arranging his uniform jacket, blowing on his brass cuff buttons, and tightening his tie to regulation tightness, Hardy strode confidently into the Commander's office to find out why he had been summoned.

Probably an important mission that only I can handle, he thought.

"Cadet Hardy, this is intolerable!" screamed Commander Dorque, angrily slamming his fist on the oak desk as Hardy entered. "This is unspeakable! Unforgivable!"

Startled by this greeting, Hardy nervously raked his hand back through his wavy blond hair. His steel-gray eyes narrowed in fear. What had he done wrong?

"What is the problem, Commander Dorque?" Beef asked, bringing himself to full, rigid attention.

"It's pronounced Dor*kay*," the headmaster corrected. "Dorkay! Please pronounce my name correctly."

"Yes, sir, Commander . . . uh Dor*kay,*" Beef stammered. He could feel tiny beads of perspiration break out on his broad, handsome forehead. "What is the matter, sir?"

"I expect all of my orders to be carried out to the fullest," Dorque said angrily, turning red as he leaned forward against his wide desk, his bald head glowing like a traffic light under the bright ceiling lights of his large, cluttered office. "To the fullest."

Beef Hardy gulped loudly. What had he done to make the old man so angry? Beef did everything he could to make the headmaster like him. He followed every Academy rule and regulation. He waited on the Commander like a servant. He even shined his plants and watered his boots for him.

Or was it the other way around?

Commander Dorque picked up a sandwich from a paper plate on his desk. "Cadet Hardy, is this the sandwich you brought from the mess for my lunch?" He waved the sandwich in the air accusingly.

"Yes, sir," Beef said reluctantly, his eyes straight ahead at attention. "That is the mess I brought you from the sandwich. I mean — that's the sandwich I made a mess with. I mean — "

The beads of perspiration on the cadet's broad forehead were the size of tennis balls now.

"Cadet Hardy, did I not ask you for a BLT sandwich?"

"Yes, you did, sir. On white bread. No crusts."

"Yes. I asked for a bacon-lettuce-tomato sandwich. And I asked you to hold the bacon and the lettuce."

"Yes, I remember, sir. You asked for a bacon-lettuce-tomato sandwich with no bacon and no lettuce."

"Correct," said the red-faced Commander wearily. He continued to wave the sandwich accusingly in the air. "But look what you brought me, Cadet Hardy."

"What, sir?"

"You brought me a tomato sandwich."

"I did?"

"Yes. Tomato on white bread."

"No crusts?"

"No crusts!" screamed Commander Dorque. "But I didn't ask for a tomato sandwich! I asked for a bacon-lettuce-tomato sandwich — without the bacon and without the lettuce!"

Commander Dorque angrily slammed the sandwich down on the wooden desk. The sandwich fell apart, and a thick, red tomato slice went flying into the air and landed on top of Beef's head with a loud plop.

Tomato juice dripped down the sides of Beef's

perfectly trimmed, regulation-length hair. He wished he could reach up and remove the tomato.

But he was standing at attention.

And the headmaster hadn't finished his tirade. "If I had wanted a tomato sandwich, I would have *asked* for a tomato sandwich!" he bellowed. "But I didn't *want* a tomato sandwich, did I?"

"Yes, sir," said Beef. "I mean, no, sir."

"I wanted a bacon-lettuce-tomato sandwich without the bacon and without the lettuce. Do you understand?"

"Yes, sir."

At this point, the door suddenly opened, and Debby Dorque, the Commander's beautiful daughter, the star of Beef Hardy's endless romantic fantasies, poked her beautiful, blue-eyed, golden-tressed head in.

"Oh. Sorry, Daddy. I didn't know you were busy."

"I'm *not*!" Commander Dorque said bitterly.

Debby floated into the room. She was carrying the camcorder she always carried as a reporter for the class video yearbook.

She looks like a *dream* in that cadet's uniform, Beef Hardy thought, allowing his eyes to follow her. She looks almost as good in her uniform as I do in mine, he admitted to himself. But I believe her shirt cuffs are an eighth of an inch too long.

He stood even more rigidly at attention, just

to impress her. He knew she was admiring the cut of his gold and gray uniform, the hard jut of his perfectly chiseled jaw, and his broad shoulders as he struck this formal military pose.

I am as straight as a department store dummy, Beef thought. No one can stand at attention like a dummy better than I can, he told himself with pride. No one!

"Daddy, why does Beef have a tomato slice on his head?" Debby Dorque asked. Her deep blue eyes filled with bewilderment.

"Uh . . . may I answer that question, sir?" Beef asked, stiffening even more.

Commander Dorque shrugged in reply.

"It's . . . uh . . . an Academy-required balancing test," Beef told Debby, thinking quickly. "Tomato balancing can be very important . . . in space. You know. When you're weightless and you need to make a sandwich . . ."

"Yes! My sandwich!" Commander Dorque suddenly remembered. "My sandwich!" His beach ball of a stomach growled so loudly it echoed.

"Daddy, you're so gross," Debby said.

"Don't call me Daddy in front of the other cadets," her father warned.

"Well, what should I call you?"

"Call me Commander Daddy."

"Commander Daddy, you're so gross," Debby repeated.

"That's better," the Commander said, beaming

at his daughter with fatherly pride. His stomach growled loudly again, causing both Debby and Beef to leap backward. The Commander's massive stomach heaved, and he grabbed it with both hands, as if trying to hold it in place.

"Go get that sandwich, Hardy!" he bellowed.

"Yes, sir!"

Since Debby was watching, Beef gave a spectacular salute, even for him, the best saluter in the entire Academy. He brought his hand up so fast and so hard to his temple that he nearly blacked out.

As his hand slapped his forehead and he staggered backward, the tomato slice slipped off the top of his head and slid under the collar of his uniform shirt. He struggled to stay at attention, but the slimy slice pressed against the back of his neck.

"You know," Commander Dorque said thoughtfully, "I've changed my mind about the sandwich." He rubbed his triple chins, a sure sign that he was thinking hard.

"Yes, sir, Commander Dorque!" cried Beef, saluting hard again, hoping it might dislodge the tomato slice and send it sliding down his back.

"That's pronounced Dor*kay*!" the headmaster corrected. "Dorkay!"

"Sorry, sir." The tomato slice clung to the back of Beef's neck, making him itch all over. He realized he was itching in places he didn't know he had! "What kind of sandwich would you like, Commander Dorque? I mean — Dorkay."

"Uh . . . let's see . . ." The Commander continued to play with his chins as he thought. "Bring me tuna fish, Swiss cheese, and tomato. On white toast."

"Okay. Very good, sir." The slimy tomato slice was sending chills down Beef's spine. He knew he *had* to get out of there before he totally *freaked* and did something that was nonregulation.

"But hold the tuna fish and the Swiss cheese," Commander Dorque ordered.

"Okay," said Beef, rolling his head from side to side, trying to dislodge the itchy tomato slice. "You want tuna fish, Swiss cheese, and tomato — without the tuna fish and Swiss cheese."

"Yes," said the headmaster. "And get it right this time. Don't bring me a tomato sandwich."

"Okay, sir. AAAACK!"

Even with his iron will, Beef just couldn't hold himself in anymore. The itching, the chills, the slimy stuff dripping down his neck were too much.

He began doing a wild dance, tossing his head from side to side, slapping furiously at the back of his neck with both hands, twisting and bending, uttering short cries of agony.

"AACK! AAACK! AACK!"

"Commander Daddy — why is Beef doing that?" Debby asked in shock and horror. She raised the camcorder to get it all on tape.

Her father shrugged, his usual response when he was confused.

"It's . . . uh . . . an ancient military salute," Beef suggested lamely, kicking his legs, tapping his boots against the floor, scratching and slapping at his back. "It was first developed by Alexander the Great — way before he became great! I read about it in my *Encyclopedia of 25,000 Military Salutes for Hands and Feet.* A book I've been memorizing for extra credit." He continued to roll his head and slap at himself.

"Cadet Hardy," the headmaster said sternly, "if I wanted to see a comedy show, I would call in those idiotic idiots known as the Space Cadets."

"Uh . . . yes, sir. AACK. AACK," croaked the desperate Beef.

"By the way, where are those four miserable excuses for cadets?"

"I believe, AACK AACK, they were, AACK AACK, having a food fight in the mess hall, sir."

The Commander smiled wistfully. "Glad to hear they decided to do something constructive for once," he said. His stomach growled and heaved. It looked at if it were trying to bounce away from him. "My sandwich! Go get my sandwich!"

"AACK. AACK. Yes, sir!" Beef tried to stand up straight, but he was itching and shivering and scratching too hard. "Uh . . . Debby, I could

9

teach you how to do this fabulous salute later, if you'd like. AACK. AACK."

She rolled her eyes and gave Beef a disgusted look.

Scrunching his head and shoulders, scratching and slapping at himself, Beef staggered out to get the Commander a tomato sandwich.

# 2

"Pull my finger," Rip said to Shaky.

The four guys known unaffectionately as the Space Cadets were finishing lunch in their exclusive corner of the mess hall, by the window. It was their exclusive corner because no one else would come near them.

"Wh-why should I?" Shaky asked suspiciously, backing away from Rip.

Shaky, who was always nervous about everything, had good reason to be nervous when sitting next to Rip at mealtime. That's because he knew Rip would eat *anything*. You don't get to weigh 300 pounds by being picky or choosey.

"Go ahead — just pull my finger," Rip insisted, holding his pointer finger in front of his nervous companion.

"Well . . ." Shaky hesitated, then reached his hand up and pulled Rip's finger.

As he pulled, Rip tilted back his head, opened

11

his mouth wide, and let out a deafening explosion of a burp that lasted at least half a minute. "Ooh, that felt good," Rip said. "Pull my finger again."

"No, thanks," Shaky said, sliding his lunch tray to the other side of the table, and quickly moving over to sit on the other side, away from Rip.

Rip laughed and began scooping more lunch into his open mouth. Andy laughed, too, a mechanical laugh that sounded somehow like a windup toy. "Ha — ha — ho — ho. . . ."

Andy was an android. A very highly developed, human-looking robot.

That was his little secret. Androids were not allowed at the Interplanetary Space Academy. But Andy wanted to be in the Space Patrol so badly, he lied about his origins.

He was passing for human.

And his pals, Shaky, Rip, and Hunk were determined to help him keep his secret.

"Yo — try to speed up your laugh a little," Hunk told Andy.

"What do you mean?" Andy asked, his dark eyes staring into Hunk's.

"You see, humans don't laugh like this," Hunk instructed. He imitated Andy's laugh: "Ha . . . Ha . . . Ha . . . Ha . . ."

Andy continued to stare at Hunk, concentrating hard in order to store Hunk's advice into his memory storage cells.

"Humans laugh like this," Hunk said. "Hahahaha."

"No, that's not right," Rip said with a mouthful of mashed potatos, brown gravy sliding down his already-food-stained chin. "That's not how humans laugh, Hunk."

"Huh?"

When in doubt, Hunk always asked "huh?" And Hunk was almost always in doubt.

With his tanned good looks, his wavy brown hair, his powerfully built body, Hunk looked like a real space hero. But, unfortunately, looks aren't everything. As Commander Dorque was always ready to point out, Hunk was a little weightless in the brains department. In fact, Hunk was about as bright as the dark side of the moon.

"Huh?" he repeated.

"Pull my finger and I'll show you how a human laughs," Rip offered.

"Huh?"

"Go ahead. Pull my finger. I'll show you — and Andy — the right way to laugh."

"D-don't d-do it," Shaky stammered.

Rip held up his pointer finger in front of Hunk. "Come on. Pull it. You want to help Andy, don't you?"

Hunk reached out and gave Rip's finger a long tug.

And as he tugged, Rip tossed his head back

13

and let out another deafening, long-distance burp.

"Gotcha," Rip said gleefully when he had finished.

"Ha . . . ha . . . ho . . . ho . . ." laughed Andy.

"They'll catch him and kick him out of the Academy if they hear Andy laugh like that," Shaky said, glancing nervously around the nearly empty mess hall to make sure no one had heard.

"Tell you what," Hunk said, admiring his own reflection in the window. He smoothed down his dark hair. "Here's a way you can practice laughing, Andy. I'll tell you a really funny joke, okay?"

"Okay," Andy said agreeably, leaning forward. He had his elbows in his lunchplate, but didn't seem to notice. "Tell me a good joke, and I'll laugh like a human."

"Well . . ." Hunk thought hard. "Here's one. What's the difference between boogers and broccoli?"

Andy thought hard. Rip put down his fork for a second.

"Hmmm . . . the difference between boogers and broccoli," Rip said thoughtfully.

"Give up?" Hunk asked. Everyone gave up. "The difference between boogers and broccoli is that Rip doesn't eat broccoli."

Hunk laughed so hard at his own joke, he fell backward off his chair, cracking his head with a loud *splat*. No one in the mess hall even bothered to look up. It happened just about every day. Hunk always had a hard time balancing in a chair for an entire meal.

Shaky tittered into his hand. Andy laughed, trying to sound human, but not really succeeding. "Ha . . . ho . . . hee . . . ha . . ."

Only Rip didn't join in the amusement. "I do *too* eat broccoli," he insisted. "I think the difference between boogers and broccoli is in the taste."

"What on earth is that green stuff you're eating right now?" Shaky asked, pointing a bony finger at Rip's overloaded plate.

"I don't know. I found it stuck under my chair," Rip said. "Not bad, though."

"Ha . . . ho . . . hee . . . ho . . ." said Andy.

"Yo — don't you ever think of anything but eating?" Hunk asked Rip, sounding exasperated. "Aren't you interested in anything else besides food?"

"Of course," Rip said. He sounded offended. "I've got other interests, you know. I've got hobbies. I'm really into sports."

"Since when is projectile vomiting considered a sport?" Hunk asked.

"Hey — I just do that vomiting across the room thing to be funny," Rip said, snorting loudly.

"Ha . . . ha . . . ho . . ." said Andy agreeably.

"Stop talking about vomiting. Please!" Shaky pleaded, holding his hand over his mouth. "I think I'm going to upchuck!"

15

"Hey — not while I'm eating," Rip said.

"Don't upchuck," Hunk told Shaky with a grin. "Toss your cookies instead."

"Don't toss your cookies," Andy said, joining in the game. "Lose your lunch."

Thinking up new ways to describe throwing up was one of their favorite games. It was the only activity at the Space Academy that they were better at than the other cadets.

"Don't lose your lunch," Rip told Shaky. "Do a Technicolor yawn!"

"Don't do a Technicolor yawn," said Hunk. "It's time for your lunch to go into reruns!"

"Pull my finger and I'll tell you a really good one," Rip said to Shaky, reaching out his pointer finger once again.

Shaky, looking positively as green as the glop on Rip's plate, stood up and started to back away from the table.

"No, really," Rip insisted. "Pull my finger. I'll tell you a great one."

Andy reached up and pulled Rip's finger. Rip burped for so long and so hard, the window in front of him steamed over.

"Ha . . . ha . . . ho . . . hee . . ." said Andy.

"What's with you guys? Space fever?" a female voice called from the other side of the room.

The four Space Cadets looked up to see Debby Dorque hurrying to their corner. "Hi, Deb," said

Hunk, lowering his voice a few octaves to impress her.

He didn't need to impress Debby. She was already totally nuts about him. She liked Hunk for his natural good looks, for his impressive muscles, for the way the light glinted in his eyes when he looked at her and said, "Huh?"

Unlike her father, Debby was fond of all four Space Cadets. Sure, they were loud and gross and fun-loving goof-offs. But she knew that, deep down inside, each of them had the makings to become loud and gross and fun-loving Space Patrolmen!

If they ever managed to graduate.

"You guys are half an hour late for Navigation Class," Debby announced.

Shaky cried out and stared at his watch, his beady, black eyes nearly popping out of his skinny face. "Oh, no! She's right!" he cried, his voice trembling. He gazed around the empty mess hall. "I thought it got awfully quiet in here."

"How can we be late?" Rip asked. "I haven't finished my lunch."

"Ha . . . ha . . . ho . . . hee . . ." Andy said. He seemed to be stuck. Hunk gave him a hard slap on the shoulder. "Thank you," Andy said with a warm grin. "Thank you . . . thank you . . . thank you . . ."

Hunk gave him another, harder slap. "Thanks.

17

I needed that," Andy said. "Ha . . . ha . . . ho . . ."

"What's wrong with him?" Debby asked suspiciously. Like everyone else in the Academy, she didn't know Andy was an android.

"He's fine. Sometimes he just has to be slapped," Hunk said, flashing her his warmest smile. His teeth shone so brightly in the mess hall light, Debby had to shield her eyes.

He's so wonderful, she thought. He's such a hunk!

"Yo! Come on, guys. Let's get to class," Hunk said, leaning on Rip's big, flabby shoulder as he pulled himself to his feet. "If we don't show up, we'll be put on report. Debby's dad has had it in for us all semester. If he catches us in here, he'll heave us all out of the Space Academy."

"Please don't say *heave,*" Shaky pleaded.

"Hunk is right about Commander Daddy," Debby quickly agreed. "Come on — hurry, guys."

Andy climbed to his feet. Rip was the only one still seated at the table.

"Come on, Rip. Hurry!" Debby pleaded. "I don't want you guys to get in trouble." She was staring meaningfully into Hunk's eyes as she said this.

Rip turned away from the table, his face dripping with food. He held up his hand to Debby. "Pull my finger and I'll get up," he said.

# 3

THE SPACE ACADEMY BUILDING was a thirty-story, glass-and-steel skyscraper located in the midst of three hundred acres of flat farmland, two hundred miles outside Des Moines, Iowa.

It was built in this remote area in the hopes that foreign spies and other evildoers would never discover it. But the gleaming skyscraper, with its spaceship hangars and enormous launching pads and landing docks, had quickly become a major tourist attraction.

Twelve months a year, cars jammed the narrow road leading to the Academy. Hot dog, ice cream, balloon, and T-shirt vendors set up carts outside the main gate. Signs for miles around proclaimed:

SECRET SPACE ACADEMY
SOUVENIRS — FREE PARKING

Inside the secret Space Academy Building, three hundred hopeful cadets lived, studied, and practiced the military and survival skills they would need in outer space. Their dream was to graduate and join the Interplanetary Space Patrol, the largest peacekeeping force in the known universe.

This year, if Commander Dorque had his way, 296 of the cadets would graduate. Four cadets — the four troublemaking slobs known as the Space Cadets — would fail miserably.

And would be executed by a firing squad. The thought brought a smile to the Commander's lips.

No. No. Even better. The four of them would be blasted into the far reaches of space, to an uninhabited planet. Left alone, just the four of them.

No. No. Something better. Something even better. Commander Dorque rested his chins in his hand and daydreamed. The four of them would be blasted into space, to a planet inhabited by man-eating, four-headed dinosaurs.

Yes. That was *pretty* good.

But was it good enough for these four walking space funguses?

These four cadets who had somehow managed to pass their first-semester courses — by cheating, no doubt — and had returned for their second semester of fumbling, of messing up, of bumbling, of having *fun — of driving Commander Dorque totally crazy!!*

How about a black hole? the weary headmaster thought, too wrapped up in his daydreams even to take a bite of the tomato sandwich sitting before him on the desk.

Yes. A black hole. There must be an endless black hole stretching to infinity that he could send them into. A black hole where they would wander in agony and terror for the rest of their lives. He'd have to check his map. There was probably a black hole nearby.

Yes, yes. He rubbed his chubby, pink hands together gleefully. That was certainly a suitable revenge. Perhaps not quite harsh enough . . .

And then Commander Dorque thought of the best revenge of all.

"I'll retire!" he cried aloud, banging his fist against his desk and squishing the tomato sandwich flat. He didn't notice. The idea was so exciting.

It's the perfect revenge, he thought. I'll retire from the Academy and leave the four of them here. I'll rent a cabin on Jupiter, maybe buy a condo on Mercury — and never see their moronic, grinning faces again.

I'll never see the fat one bending over and ripping his $20,000 space suit from stem to stern. Or sneezing in the weightless chamber and chasing his own snot around in circles.

I'll never have to see the one who's always grinning at me and beeping. Always making that annoying beeping sound and saying things that don't make any sense. What's his problem, anyway? If I wanted a beeping cadet, I'd bring in an android!

And the shaky one. He makes me nervous just looking at him. He'd make *anyone* nervous. He's an accident waiting to happen.

And the really handsome one. Their leader. Hunk. The one who doesn't know his elbow from Uranus! The one with a brain like a moon rock.

The one my daughter is so nuts about . . .

What did Debby see in him, anyway? Why couldn't she like someone sensible, someone worthy, someone outstanding, someone with a real future — like Beef Hardy?

The Commander smiled at the thought of Beef Hardy. Hardy was such an obedient servant, such a weak-willed teacher's pet, such a goody-goody, such a simpering, fawning, brown-nosing slave.

In other words, the perfect cadet.

So why wasn't Debby attracted to him?

Oh, well, it didn't matter anymore, he decided, the smile returning to his lips. It didn't matter because he was going to retire from the Academy.

Right now.

He pushed down a button on his office intercom. "Miss Moon, please get me General Innis Outt at Space Patrol Headquarters."

"Yes, Commander Dorque."

"It's Dor*kay*!" he shouted. "Dor*kay*!"

"Sorry, sir. You said you wished to speak to Miss Moon?"

"No," the Commander said, exasperated. "*You* are Miss Moon. I wish to speak to General Innis Outt."

"Okay, okay. You don't have to shout."

Commander Dorque took a deep breath. I won't have to deal with Miss Moon anymore, either, he thought. She wasn't bad as far as secretaries went. But she had never learned to type. Or take dictation. Or answer the phone. Or take messages.

Aside from those few defects, she was a pretty good secretary, he decided. If only she would learn to wear deodorant . . .

He tapped his chubby fingers on the wooden desk, waiting for the call to his superior officer to go through. Dorque knew General Outt wouldn't be happy about his decision to retire. He'd be a hard man to replace, he had to admit. It would probably take two men to fill his boots, Dorque decided. Or maybe three or four.

But too bad. He was retiring. Leaving. Getting out. *Escaping!* His mind was made up.

The intercom buzzed, surprising him out of his pleasant daydreams. "Your call is ready," Miss Moon's voice informed him.

Commander Dorque picked up the phone receiver. He took a deep breath and prepared to break the news to his commanding officer. "Hello, General?"

"This is General Inn's office," said a young woman's voice.

"General Inn?"

"No, I'm sorry," the woman told him, "General Inn is out."

"General Innis Outt? Please let me speak to him."

"I'm sorry, sir. General Inn is out."

"Yes. General Innis Outt. Put him on, please."

"I can't, sir. General Inn is out."

"I know, I know. General Innis Outt. That's who I'd like to speak to. Please — connect me at once."

"How can I?" the woman asked, her voice becoming sharp.

"It's quite easy. It's your job, isn't it?" Commander Dorque shouted. He was also beginning to lose his patience.

"I'm trying to tell you, sir, that General Inn is out," she repeated.

"And I'm trying to tell you that's who I'm trying to reach."

"But you can't reach him if he's out."

"Out? Who is out?" Dorque bellowed.

"General Inn. I told you. He's out."

Commander Dorque wiped perspiration off his

bald head with his open palm. "General Innis Outt?"

"Yes."

"Let me speak to him."

"General Inn is out."

"Yes!" Dorque cried. "That's him!"

"But he's out!" she screamed.

"Who is out?" Dorque realized he was becoming confused.

"The General," she replied.

"General Innis Outt?"

"That's what I've been trying to tell you," she cried.

"Well, then, put him on," Dorque said.

He heard a loud scream on the other end of the line. Then her voice returned with forced calmness. "I'm sorry, sir. I cannot connect you to General Inn. General Inn is out. Perhaps I could connect you with General Outt."

"General Innis Outt?" Dorque asked.

"Yes, sir. For the two-hundredth time. General Inn is out. I'm going to connect you to General Innis Outt now. Okay?"

"Yes, yes! Please!" cried the exhausted Commander. "Please — I beg of you. Connect me to General Outt."

"The man is a total idiot," he heard the woman say to someone in her office.

Who is she talking about? Dorque wondered.

There was a loud buzz, followed by silence on the line, followed by another loud buzz. He switched the phone to his other ear.

A different, very shrill woman's voice came on the line. "General Outt," she said.

"Is he in?" Commander Dorque asked.

"You want General Inn?"

"Yes, I want to know if the General is in," Dorque said impatiently.

"You wish to speak to General Inn?"

"Yes, I wish to speak to the General if he's in," Dorque told her.

"Well, this is General Outt's office," the woman said, her voice growing even shriller.

"Yes, General Innis Outt," Dorque said.

"General Inn is out? I didn't know that, sir. Shall I tell that to General Outt?"

"I — wish — to — speak — to — General — Outt," Dorque said, pronouncing each word slowly and distinctly. "Is he in or out?"

"General Innoroutt? He is out," the voice said. "All three Generals are on assignment, sir. General Inn is out, General Outt is out, General Innoroutt is out. But he'll be in soon with General Later."

"Sooner or later?"

"General Later will be in sooner than General Sooner, sir. General Sooner always comes in later than General Later. Would you care to leave a message?"

26

"Never mind," Dorque said, and weakly hung up the phone.

He decided to write General Outt a letter.

He pushed a button on his intercom. "Miss Moon, take a letter, please."

After a brief, thoughtful silence, Miss Moon's voice came back on the small speaker. "Yes, sir. Where shall I take it?"

"No, no. I mean, please come into my office and let me dictate a letter to you."

"I'm sorry, Commander. I don't know how. Please don't make me feel bad because I have no secretarial skills. I'm a very sensitive person, and I don't like to be constantly reminded that I have no skills or abilities."

"I'm sorry, Miss Moon. Very sorry," Dorque apologized.

"Just because I can't do anything," she said, starting to sob, "doesn't mean I'm not a good person or a good secretary."

"You're right. You're absolutely right," he said. He could hear her sobbing through the door to the outer office. "Miss Moon — please. Is there anything I can do?"

"Well . . . can I have a raise?" she asked.

"Yes, certainly. Excellent idea," he said. "Now as to that letter, I'll write it myself. Please bring me a pen and some stationery."

"I'm sorry, sir. I don't know where they're located."

"In the top cabinet drawer," Dorque said impatiently.

"I don't know which cabinet," she said, starting to sob again.

"The cabinet on the left," he told her, sighing.

"The cabinet on the left?"

"Right."

"The cabinet on the right?" she asked, confused.

"No — left! Left! LEFT!!" he screamed into the square intercom.

"The cabinet on the left is locked, sir. I don't know how to unlock it."

At that moment, the phone rang. Startled, Commander Dorque picked it up. "Hello?"

"Yes, hello, Donald," said a familiar man's voice.

"Dor*kay*," the Commander corrected. "It's pronounced Dor*kay*."

"But I was using your first name. Your first name is Donald, is it not?" said the voice into Dorque's ear.

Suddenly the Commander recognized the voice. "General Outt!" he exclaimed. "Are you in?"

"No, I'm out. Inn is out, Innorout is out, and I'm out. But I received a message that you called. What can I do for you, Donald?"

"Well, General Outt, I've decided to retire from the Academy."

The laughter on the other end was long and loud. Dorque could tell from the sound of it that Outt had tears in his eyes from laughing so hard.

"Does this mean you don't want me to retire?" Dorque asked, his voice trembling with disappointment.

"No, no. You can retire, by all means," Outt said enthusiastically. "Of course you can retire, Donald — as soon as you get rid of those four weirdo cadets in your freshman class."

Commander Dorque wasn't certain he was hearing correctly. "Get rid of them?"

"Yes. Get rid of them," Outt said firmly. "As long as those four are in your school, no one in his right mind will take your job."

"You mean — "

"I mean I won't be able to replace you until those four Space Cadets are gone."

The headmaster was beginning to catch on. Maybe this wasn't such disappointing news after all. "You mean I should have them killed?" he asked hopefully.

There was a brief silence at the other end. "That's not a good idea. I believe that's still against the law," General Outt told him.

"Pity," said Dorque thoughtfully.

"The four Space Cadets must either graduate or flunk out before you retire, Donald," General Outt said. "I've got to go now. Inn just came in. I don't want him to know that I'm out."

He hung up, leaving the Commander to ponder his words. Graduate or flunk out . . . graduate or flunk out . . .

Graduate? Graduate?! There was no way those four morons would ever graduate. If Dorque had to wait for them to graduate, he'd be a doddering old man, totally deranged, drooling down his chin.

Dorque wiped the saliva off his chin and thought hard.

There was no choice in the matter. The four Space Cadets *had* to flunk out.

Semester exams were coming up. It was the perfect opportunity to make sure they flunked.

A thoughtful smile slowly crossed the headmaster's flabby face. He had a plan. A foolproof plan. He buzzed the intercom. "Miss Moon, please ask Cadet Hardy to come to my office at once," he said.

"I don't know how, sir," came back the reply.

# 4

RIP BOUNCED INTO THE CLASSROOM, still burping from lunch. Seeing that his usual seat was taken, he plopped down in the first empty seat he saw. The chair squeaked in protest as Rip's three hundred pounds landed on it.

He and his three friends had been too late for Navigation Class, so they had gone directly to their next class, The History of Rocket Fuel. Most cadets considered this an extremely boring class, but it was one of Rip's favorites.

It was one of his favorites because it was taught be Corporal Alice Powderoffski. Corporal Powderoffski, or Powder, as the cadets secretly called her, was very pretty, with a delicate, heart-shaped face, dramatic black eyes, and straight, black hair swept back past her shoulders.

But she wasn't a very good instructor. For one thing, she was very nervous. Her nervousness made her constantly drop things — her pens, her pointer, her lecture notes.

And every time she turned her back and bent down to pick up what she had dropped, Rip would quickly raise the back of his hand to his lips, press his lips against his hand, and blow really hard, making a truly gross sound.

The sound would cause Corporal Powderoffski to leap a foot in the air, turn bright red, spin around angrily to face the crowded classroom, and demand, "Okay — who's the wise guy?"

She never figured out who was making the rude noise.

Which was why this was one of Rip's favorite classes.

Rip looked around the large lecture hall as Corporal Powderoffski stepped behind the lectern to begin her lecture. Her subject was "Uses of Hydrogen By-Products by Other Planets." Cadets were earnestly taking notes. Rip wondered why.

Rip saw Hunk in the front row, scrunched low in his chair, his eyes closed, already beginning to snore loudly even though the class had just begun. Rip smiled. Good old Hunk. He never let a class interfere with his sleep.

Shaky was a couple of rows behind Hunk. He was nervously writing down every word Powder said. What a waste of time, Rip thought. Shaky always took pages and pages of notes. But he couldn't read his own handwriting. Every night, he'd struggle to read what he had written, give up, and throw his notes in the trash.

Shaky hadn't passed a single exam all semester. But he had come very close once. And he claimed his near-success was because he took such good notes.

Andy, who was a few seats to the left, was grinning at Rip, obviously not paying any more attention than Rip was. Suddenly Andy beeped loudly.

I wish he would stop that, Rip thought. That beeping twice every hour on the hour and half hour is going to give him away.

Rip wondered if all of Andy's bolts had been properly tightened. Sometimes he acted as if he had a screw loose.

Corporal Powderoffski picked up her pointer and started to move to a large universe map behind her. Rip readied himself. He knew it was just about time for him to get into gear.

Yes!

She dropped her pointer. It clattered noisily to the floor.

Rip took a deep breath.

She turned her back and bent down to pick it up.

Rip blew hard against the back of his hand. The rude noise filled the large classroom. Everyone laughed.

Corporal Powderoffski leaped into the air, turned bright red, spun around, and demanded,

"Okay — who's the wise guy?" Her face still the color of a ripe tomato, she folded her slender arms in front of her and glanced from face to face. "You're not funny, you know," she said angrily. Shaking her head, she turned and bent over again to retrieve her pointer from the floor.

Rip turned in time to see Andy go into action, copying Rip, as usual. Andy raised the back of his hand to his lips, blew as hard as he could and — blew his hand off!

"Quick — hide it! Hide it!" Rip cried in a loud whisper, gesturing wildly to Andy.

Andy, looking very confused, picked up his loose hand with his still-attached hand and held it up to study it. Several colored wires hung out from the wrist.

"Put it away! Put it away!" Rip urged.

Andy glanced over at Rip. He raised the hand up. He grinned at Rip, and tossed the hand to him.

Rip had to jump up to catch it. "Are you crazy?" he whispered to Andy, who just grinned back at him.

"What is going on back there?" Corporal Powderoffski demanded, staring directly at Rip.

"No problem. Really. No problem," Rip said, quickly hiding the hand behind his back.

"What have you got behind your back?" the instructor asked.

"Nothing. Really," Rip told her, sitting back down, the hand still behind him.

"I was just giving him a hand," Andy offered.

"Will you knock it off?" Rip whispered.

"I didn't knock it off. I blew it off," Andy said.

"Rip — perhaps you'd like to share what you have behind your back with the rest of the class," Powder suggested.

"Uh . . . I don't think so," Rip said.

"Come on. Share it with us," Powder urged.

"No. Really. It's just a human hand," Rip said.

"A human hand?" The instructor laughed scornfully. "You can make up a better story than that."

"No. Really. That's what it is," Rip said, hoping the honest approach would get him out of this jam. "Just a human hand."

"Well, I can't take up any more class time with this foolishness," Powder said, exasperated. "Especially since we have a special guest speaker today. Now, where was I?" She forgot about Rip and resumed her lecture.

Rip breathed a sigh of relief. That was a close one. He tucked Andy's hand into his notebook and pretended to pay attention to what Corporal Powderoffski was saying.

A few minutes later, the instructor called Shaky up to the front of the class and handed him the pointer. "Please trace a line on the universe map through the Inter-Cooperative Rocket Fuel Trading Planets," she demanded.

"Do I have to?" Shaky was trembling all over. He hated standing up in front of the entire class.

Corporal Powderoffski nodded. Yes, he had to.

Shaky took the pointer in his shaking hands and poked himself in the eye with it. "Ow! I'm blind! I'm blind!"

"You're okay," Powder said, making an annoyed face. "Just trace a line."

With the injured eye shut tight, Shaky turned to the map, raised the pointer in his trembling hand, drew it across the map, and tore the map right down the middle. He lurched forward and grabbed the map, trying to hold it together, and the whole thing fell off the wall and onto the floor at his feet.

"S-sorry," he stammered, handing back the pointer.

"Nice work," Corporal Powderoffski said sarcastically.

She bent over to pick the map up, and Rip immediately made his rude noise. The classroom erupted in laughter.

This is a *great* class, Rip thought.

"I believe it's time to introduce our special guest," Powder said, deciding to leave the torn map on the floor. "I know that you will treat our guest more considerately than you treat me."

Hunk, sound asleep right in front of her, let out a loud snort and shifted his long legs without waking up.

"Our guest speaker today comes all the way from the planet Pluto," Powder told them.

This should be fun, thought Rip. I love those little blue Plutonians. They're so cute. They look like round blue bugs.

"He is the Plutonian Minister of Rocket Fuel Consumer Affairs, and he is going to tell us about the history of rocket fuel on Pluto," Powder announced. "I'm sure you'll be very interested in what he has to tell you." She gestured to the back of the room. "Minister Pajarajaja, would you come up to the front, please?"

All of the cadets turned to the back to see the Plutonian Minister. But no one stood up.

"Minister Pajarajaja, are you still here?" Powder asked, shielding her eyes with her hand to see the back of the vast classroom. "I saw you sitting back there at the start of the class, and . . ."

There was no reply. No little blue Plutonian stepped forward.

"That's strange," said the instructor, clearly surprised. "The Minister was sitting right over — " Her mouth dropped open as she pointed right at Rip.

"What?" Rip cried. "Why is everyone looking at me?"

"He was sitting in your seat, Rip," Powder said, her eyes wide with horror.

Rip jumped up and looked behind him. "Hey — what's this blue stuff stuck to the back of my pants?"

Everyone groaned. Corporal Powderoffski turned as white as the close-up map of the moon behind her.

"The Minister!" she shrieked. "You sat on the Minister!"

That explains the squeak when I sat down, Rip thought. He pulled the sticky blue stuff off his pants and held it up to examine it. It looked like a pancake made of blue Silly Putty. But it had two eyes and a mouth and was carrying a briefcase.

The room erupted in cries of horror and disgust. Several cadets were heaving their lunches onto the floor. Shaky had passed out.

"The Minister! You've squashed the Minister!" Corporal Powderoffski was screaming hysterically. "This could mean *war*!!"

"Uh . . . is this going to affect my grade?" Rip asked.

# 5

"YES, YES. THE MINISTER will be returned to you at once," Commander Dorque said into the phone, wiping the perspiration off his forehead with an already-damp handkerchief. "We are so sorry about this unfortunate accident. We are sparing no expense to return him to Pluto."

The angry voice at the other end shouted something the Commander couldn't quite understand. The connection between Earth and Pluto was not the best.

"Yes. We have folded the Minister up and sealed him in an envelope. We're dropping him in the mail right now. I'm sending him airmail. You will have him back in a few weeks." Dorque wiped his forehead again. "Yes, I wrote 'Do Not Bend' on the envelope. You should be able to revive him quickly. He's a little flat, but he's still breathing."

After several more apologies, he hung up.

Those Space Cadets cause me nothing but trouble, he thought, angrily squeezing the edge of his desk. Imagine — sitting on the Plutonian Minister! That's not just careless, it's — it's *irresponsible!*

I must get rid of the four of them. I *must!*

The headmaster was dreaming up ways to eliminate the Space Cadets, ways that didn't seem quite painful enough to him, when Cadet Beef Hardy strode jauntily into the office, his toothy smile at a regulation 35-degree lip-width, his blond hair trimmed to follow cadet grooming rules, his gold and gray uniform pressed smooth as granite.

"Good afternoon, Commander," Hardy said. "You're looking really well. That red tie certainly brings out the color of your cheeks. Are you doing something new with your scalp? It looks particularly shiny today. And how is your lovely daughter? Has she mentioned me lately?"

"I'm in no mood for chitchat," Dorque said, pushing his chair back from the big wooden desk and standing up to his full height — four feet, six inches (in his boots). He stepped around the desk, collided with the wastebasket, which was just a little taller than he, and began to pace nervously back and forth the length of the office.

Cadet Hardy stood at attention facing the now-empty desk. "I heard about the splat, sir," he said softly.

"The splat?"

"Yes. You know. The Plutonian Minister. The splat."

The headmaster made a sour face. "Yes, yes. The splat. I suppose the news is all over the Academy by now."

"Well . . . that fat cadet named Rip is showing everyone the blue stain the Minister made on his uniform pants."

"Enough!" Dorque cried, holding up a hand as if to hold Hardy back. "Enough!"

"Sorry, sir." No wonder the Commander was in a bad mood. Sitting on foreign ministers was against Regulations 455–X and 455–Y.

"I need your help, Cadet Hardy," Commander Dorque said, lowering his voice and looking from side to side to make sure no one was watching.

"You need another sandwich, sir?" Hardy asked.

"No, no. Forget about sandwiches." Dorque hoisted himself up onto the front of his desk. His feet dangled over the edge, a good foot from the floor. "Although, I could go for a tuna fish, lettuce, and tomato on white bread, without the tuna fish and without the lettuce. . . . No. Forget it. This is more important than sandwiches. Semester exams are coming up — right?"

"Right, sir," Hardy said. "I've been studying day and night, sir. I know I'll finish at the head of my class, maybe even higher."

"Good for you," the Commander said dryly. "But that's not what I'm worried about right now. What I'm worried about is that the fat cadet and his three good-for-nothing buddies might not flunk out."

"No chance of that, sir," Hardy reassured him with a smile. "They're failing every course. They're even failing Lunch — *and* they're failing Bathroom."

"They're failing Bathroom?" Dorque asked.

"Don't make me go into detail," Hardy said quietly. "I really don't think there's a chance they'll pass, sir."

"That's what I thought last semester," Dorque said miserably. "But somehow they managed to pass enough courses to stay in school."

"They cheated, Commander Dorque. I'm sure of it," Hardy said.

"It's pronounced Dor*kay*," Dorque reminded him. "Dor*kay*." He leaned forward on the edge of the desk and spoke in a low whisper. "I need to make sure they fail this time, Hardy. I don't want any slipups. I want them out of my Academy — all four of them. And I want you to help make sure that they fail."

Cadet Hardy gave a brain-splitting salute that sent him staggering backward. "Anything you say, sir," he said, shaking his head to clear away all the sparkling stars he was seeing. "I'm always ready and willing to help. Perhaps I could get together with your daughter tonight and make a plan to — ”

“Leave my daughter out of it,” Dorque said quickly. “She's sweet on that cadet named Hunk.”

“She is?” Cadet Hardy's perfect, bronze tan faded just a bit at this news.

“If Debby gets wind of any of this, she'll try to help the Space Cadets,” Dorque said, and then added through clenched teeth, “the little traitor.”

“Perhaps I can make her see the big mistake she's making,” Hardy said, somewhat desperately. “Perhaps if I were assigned to sit next to her in all of her classes and in the mess hall, I could — ”

The headmaster silenced Hardy with a stern shake of his head. He leaned forward a little more on his desktop and said, “Think of someone else to help you, Hardy. Someone who loathes and despises the four Space Cadets as much as we do.” He leaned forward a bit more, waiting in silent anticipation.

Cadet Hardy furrowed his brow and struck a thoughtful pose. “I think Cadet Cheesewell might be willing to help, sir.”

Cadet Camembert (or Cammy) Cheesewell was the best-looking female cadet in the Space Academy. She had flaming red hair, and sparkling emerald-green eyes. She wore her uniform so tight, she couldn't walk, and had to be carried from class to class.

A look of surprise covered Commander Dorque's face. "Cammy Cheesewell? Why does she dislike the Space Cadets?"

"Well . . . they're always whistling at her, sir. You know. Always chasing her down the halls, making jokes about how tight her uniform is. Stuff like that. Cammy hates stuff like that. She says it's sexist and rude."

The headmaster leaned forward a bit more, thinking about Cammy Cheesewell. "I knew her father," he confided. "Muenster Cheesewell. He and I were buddies during the Martian Wars. Poor fellow. Got his head cut off."

"During a battle with Martians?" Hardy asked.

"No. Trying to open a can of beans. He just couldn't get the hang of an electric can opener. He thought you had to hold it up in front of you. Before we knew what was happening, he'd got his head caught in it, and" — Commander Dorque shook his head sadly and sighed — "never did get the can of beans open. They were kidney beans. My favorite."

"Sad," Hardy said, looking down and admiring his own reflection in his perfectly shined boots.

"So you and Cadet Cheesewell will help make sure that the four Space Cadets flunk their exams?" Dorque asked, returning to his concern of the moment.

"We'll try, sir," Hardy said, starting to give

another head-banging salute, but catching him-self just in time.

"Trying isn't good enough," Dorque said. "I'm counting on you, Hardy." And then he added in a whisper, "I'll make it worth your while."

"You will, sir?" Hardy said, suddenly breathing hard, his tongue hanging out like an expectant golden retriever.

"I'll let you have a ten percent discount at the Academy Gift and Souvenir Shop," Dorque announced grandly.

Cadet Hardy's shoulders slumped. He looked very disappointed. "Only ten percent?"

"Okay. Make it twelve percent," Dorque said irritably, leaning forward a bit more on the edge of the desk. "On all items except clothing. I might even throw in a date with my daughter — if the Space Cadets fail miserably."

"Don't worry about a thing, sir," Cadet Hardy said, already thinking about what to wear to impress Debby Dorque on their date. *Perhaps a gold bandanna draped casually around my neck,* he thought. *He'd have to check the dress code book and see if it was allowed. . . .*

"I am worried. Very worried," Commander Dorque confided. "You *must* succeed in getting them to fail." He leaned forward a bit more, toppled off the desk, and fell flat on his face on the floor.

# 6

"Can I peel that watermelon for you?" Cammy Cheesewell asked Beef Hardy.

"You don't peel a slice of watermelon," Hardy said, moving a few inches away from her.

She scooted her chair closer to him, her green eyes sparkling with eagerness. "Can I spit out the seeds for you?"

Beef Hardy made a face. "I think I'd probably better spit out my own seeds."

She scooted a bit closer. Her wavy, red hair was right in his face now, making it very hard to eat the watermelon. "Could I chew on the rind a bit. You know, soften it up for you?"

"I don't like soft rinds," he said impatiently.

"I just want to be helpful," she said, pouting.

The truth was, Cammy Cheesewell had dreamed for months about a night like this. Alone in the mess hall with her dream cadet. Watching him eat watermelon and spit the seeds across the room.

The other cadets were such childish clods, Cammy thought. But Cadet Hardy had style.

She pounded his back as he started to sputter and choke, and after only five or six hard pounds, the seed that had lodged in his throat came flying out of his mouth.

She wiped his chin for him, and tucked the napkin into her knapsack. A keepsake of this, their first date together.

Hardy looked into her eager, green eyes and thought about Debby Dorque. He wished it were Debby sitting here in the mess, watching him choke on watermelon seeds.

Where is Debby right now? he wondered. Off somewhere with that big hunk Hunk?

Thinking about it made him mad.

"So, are you clear on the plan?" he asked Cammy.

She nodded, her red lips tightening in seriousness.

"You're sure you can get the itching powder from the supply room?" he asked.

She nodded again. "Of course. I have supply-room duty after class three days a week."

"And you're sure you want to help?" Hardy demanded.

"Yes," she said, her voice a confidential whisper. "Those Space Cadets are a disgrace to the school. They don't take anything seriously. They don't even take fighting and maiming and killing seriously. Can you imagine how terrible it would be if they graduated and got into the Space Patrol?"

"So you're with me on this mission?" Beef asked, accidentally biting off a piece of the rind, grimacing at its sourness.

"I'm with you all the way!" Cammy exclaimed, slapping him enthusiastically on the back, sending another volley of seeds flying from his mouth across the room.

"It's exam time. Got to hit the books!" Hunk declared.

Andy picked up a textbook from the shelf and hit it as hard as he could with his recently repaired hand. "Studying is fun," he said. "Ha . . . ha . . . ho . . . hee . . ."

It was an hour past lights-out — 2200 hours, to be exact. The four Space Cadets were sitting around their cluttered dorm room, thinking of new ways to avoid studying.

Dinner in the mess hall had been followed by a brief lecture given by Commander Dorque on the subject of why cadets should not sit on visiting ministers. The Commander had informed them that the whole unfortunate incident was being investigated to see if it would be necessary to discipline the guilty cadet.

At this point, Rip had jumped to his feet and asked if anyone knew how to get a blue stain out of uniform pants. The hall had erupted in laughter, and Commander Dorque quickly disappeared through a side exit.

The Space Cadets had spent the rest of the evening in the rec room, holding a long-distance sneezing competition. Standing against one wall of the brightly lit room, the cadets tried to sneeze across the room to a target on the opposite wall.

Andy won easily, for distance and for accuracy. Hunk came in second, but he had to quit when, after a twenty yarder, he suddenly came down with a nosebleed.

All four cadets then hurried out of the rec room before someone made them clean the wall.

Now it was time to get down to some serious studying. Their first exam was in the morning.

"Hey — remember the time we had to take a physical, and Shaky stayed up all night studying for his urine test?" Hunk said, laughing.

Rip and Andy laughed, too.

"What's so funny about that?" Shaky demanded. "I *passed* it, didn't I?!" He walked over to the desk and pulled out his notebook, which was crammed with the notes he had taken in class. "You guys are just jealous because I have notes to study and you don't."

Hunk reached over and grabbed the notebook away from him. "Now *I* have notes to study," he said.

Shaky tried to grab them back, but Hunk tossed the notebook to Andy.

"Give those back!" Shaky cried, tripping over a chair as he scrambled frantically to get it away from Andy. He made a wild grab, but Andy passed the notebook to Rip.

The pass went high, and the notebook, some of its pages fluttering out, sailed over Rip's head and landed in the fish tank.

"No!" Shaky cried. He lunged toward the fish tank, but Rip stuck a foot out, and Shaky went flying onto the carpet. Rip pulled the sopping wet notes out of the tank.

"Pass 'em! Pass 'em!" Hunk called.

"Go out for a long one!" Rip cried, and heaved the notebook across the room to Hunk.

Hunk dived over the couch and made a one-handed grab. Shaky climbed to his feet and, with a loud groan, leaped at Hunk, his arms outstretched.

"Give me my notes!"

He grabbed the notebook and pulled. Hunk pulled, too. They tore the notebook in two, the soaked pages falling to the floor.

"I've got 'em!" Rip yelled. He dived for the pages, knocking the fish tank off its table. The tank shattered, and a flood of water and goldfish rushed over the carpet.

All four Space Cadets were scrambling around on the wet carpet, wrestling, splashing, laughing, tossing goldfish back and forth, tearing up the remains of Shaky's notes, all soaking wet, when Debby Dorque knocked on the door and quickly stepped into the room.

"What on earth are you guys doing?" she asked.

"Uh . . . well . . . we're studying," Hunk told her.

Commander Dorque tightened the belt on his maroon bathrobe as he stepped out into the dimly lit corridor. Even though it was the middle of the night, several hours after lights-out, he looked both ways to make sure no one was watching.

Why am I sneaking around like this? he asked himself. I *am* the commanding officer here, after all.

Trying not to make a sound, he turned the corner, his fuzzy blue bedroom slippers padding silently as he cautiously made his way toward the kitchen.

He knew very well why he was sneaking around. He was sneaking around because he didn't want to be caught by Carmella Flan, the school cook. Carmella Flan, Commander of the Kitchen.

Carmella Flan.

Even her name sounded delicious to Commander Dorque.

But even more delicious than her name was

her cherry-rhubarb pie. The headmaster could not resist her cherry-rhubarb pie. He thought about it constantly — while reading the morning orders, while instructing his staff, while sitting at his desk staring up at the ceiling. He even dreamed about it.

And on some nights — nights like this one — he wasn't content just to think about the pie of his dreams. He had to have a slice. Or four.

The only problem was that Carmella Flan was very protective of her pies. She had rules for her kitchen. And one of the rules at the top of her list was that no pies should be disturbed in the middle of the night by anyone — not even pie-crazed Space Academy headmasters.

Carmella Flan protected her cherry-rhubarb pies as if they were gold bullion. She would have padlocked each pie, if it were possible to padlock pie.

To put it in food terms, Carmella Flan was one tough cookie. Her name might sound soft and custardy. But Carmella was as hard as Dutch pretzels.

Which is why the Commander of the Inter-planetary Space Academy was creeping down the hall to the kitchen on tiptoe in his fuzzy slippers, stopping to glance nervously behind him at each turn in the corridor.

Then, taking a deep breath, he pushed open

the kitchen door cautiously and stepped inside without turning on a light. A small night-light cast a narrow cone of yellow light down on the floor beside the massive, metal refrigerator. But Commander Dorque didn't need to see. His feet knew the way to the pie pantry.

I can taste it already, he thought.

The sweet, soft cherries. The tangy tartness of the rhubarb. The dark, syrupy filling. The butter-light crust, so firm yet so flaky.

Even in the darkness, it took the Commander only a few seconds to locate a cherry-rhubarb on the shelf full of pies and pull it into his arms. A few seconds after that, he had found a fork in the silverware bin against the wall.

A few seconds after that, he was noisily, greed-ily, gleefully satisfying his mad pie desire in the darkness. Forkful followed forkful. It was even more delicious than he had remembered.

Were there tears in his eyes? Yes, of course. He was a sensitive man, sensitive to the work of a true pie artist!

When I retire after this semester, he thought, gulping down a huge, delicious hunk without taking the time to chew, I will have to take Carmella Flan with me.

Yes! Why hadn't he thought of it before?

He would ask Carmella Flan to marry him. And then the two of them would retire from the

Academy, go off to a quiet planet to bake and eat endless cherry-rhubarb pies together in wedded bliss.

The headmaster was still planning and gobbling, gobbling and planning when the kitchen lights suddenly clicked on. He continued to chew, squinting against the brightness to see who had entered.

"Carmella!"

She stood in her rotund glory, her bleached orange hair down to her shoulders, meeting the high collar of her pink flannel nightdress. Her normally beady blue eyes flared angrily. Smoke seemed to pour from her rather lengthy nose. Her mouth was a dark, gaping hole of surprise and anger.

"Carmella!" he repeated, quickly shoveling in another forkful of pie.

Her greeting was not exactly friendly. "Thief!" she cried.

"Carmella — what a pleasant surprise!" Commander Dorque recovered quickly from his shock. His plans of marriage were still fresh in his mind. "I was just thinking of you!"

"Thief!" she repeated. "Put down that pie."

"Carmella, my dear, dear Carmella," he said grandly, holding on tightly to the beloved pie, although it was already half eaten. "Carmella, do not be angry with me. I have something to say to you, something important."

This seemed to throw her off-guard. "Go ahead. Speak." She still glared at him with fury.

Commander Dorque decided to tell her what was in his heart, to tell her of his feeling for her and her pies, of his plans to retire with her and go off somewhere where she could bake hundreds of pies for him in peaceful wedded bliss.

He opened his mouth to tell her of all this.

But instead of the golden words he had planned, what first came out was a thunderous, stomach-quaking, earsplitting burp.

Whereupon Carmella Flan uttered a cry of rage, hoisted up an enormous bronze frying pan, and began swinging it wildly in front of her.

Commander Dorque wisely gave up any further attempts at proposing, and fled for his life.

# 7

"GOOD MORNING, HUNK," Debby Dorque called as they hurried through the crowded corridor. She was holding up her camcorder, as usual, busily recording the first morning of exams for the video yearbook.

"Yo," Hunk replied, yawning.

"Hunk — why is your cap on backward?" she asked.

"How do you know it's on backward? I haven't decided which way I'm going yet," he said.

She couldn't decide whether he was joking or not, so she decided to ignore it. He's so hand-some, she thought. It's too bad he can't dress himself.

The hallway was much quieter than usual. Most cadets had been up the whole night, studying for their first exam. "Oops. Forgot Shaky," Hunk said, slapping his handsome forehead.

"Forgot him?" Debby looked confused.

"Yeah. I promised I'd carry him to class this morning."

"Carry him? Why?"

"Exams make him a little nervous. He forgets how to walk."

"Forgets?" Debby stopped and turned to face Hunk. "Forgets how to walk?"

"Just at exam time. They make him real nervous. He forgets how to walk, how to talk, how to go to the bathroom — everything."

Debby shifted the camcorder in her hand. "Well, if he forgets *everything,* how does he ever pass his exams?"

"He doesn't," Hunk said, smiling for some reason. "He always flunks. That's why exams make him so nervous."

It all seemed logical to Hunk, so Debby assumed it made sense somehow. They started walking again.

"Poor guy," Hunk continued, still talking about Shaky. "Sometimes his arms and legs just shake all over. It's scary."

"That's terrible," Debby said. "It would be hard to go through life always being so nervous like that." They walked a little further, and then Debby asked, "What does Shaky want to be when he graduates and gets into the Space Patrol?"

"He wants to be on the bomb disarming squad," Hunk said.

*   *   *

Hunk carried Shaky into the vast gymnasium that was serving as an exam hall and set him down near the back. "What exam is this?" Shaky stammered. "I've forgotten."

"It's a simple one," Hunk said reassuringly. "It's a Discipline Exam. Piece of cake. You'll ace it, Shaky."

"What does that mean?" Shaky asked shakily, pulling nervously at Hunk's jacket sleeve. "I forget."

"Look, man, this exam is nothing at all. You just have to stand at attention for an hour. You know, to show you've got discipline."

"What? What did you just say? I forget," Shaky said.

Hunk turned and greeted Andy and Rip, who were standing in the row in front of him. "Yo, Andy — how's it going?"

Andy beeped loudly. "Correct time is oh-nine hundred hours and four minutes," he said, grinning.

Uh-oh, thought Hunk. Some of his memory chips must be damaged or something. How's he ever going to pass this exam if he's beeping and giving the correct time every minute?

Rip was eating as usual. He had a banana in his mouth.

"Yo, Rip — " Hunk called.

"I can't hear you," Rip called back. "I've got a

banana in my mouth!" He laughed uproariously.

Hunk didn't get the joke.

"Ha . . . ha . . . hee . . . ho . . ." Andy laughed, too.

Then he beeped and gave the time and temperature.

Out in the corridor, Beef Hardy was striding purposefully toward the gym to meet Cammy Cheesewell and go over their plan to make the four Space Cadets fail.

Hardy stopped just outside the entrance where a cadet plebe named Smithers gave him an enthusiastic salute. Hardy returned the salute. Then his lightning-fast hand shot out, grabbed Smithers' ear, and twisted it between his fingers until it made a cracking noise and faced the wrong way.

"Ow!" cried the plebe, raising a hand gingerly to his throbbing ear. "Why'd you do that, sir?"

"Just testing," Hardy sneered. "You don't mind if I test my finger strength on your head, do you, plebe?"

"No, sir," moaned Smithers, his eyes shut tight in pain.

"I believe your ear is facing the wrong way," Hardy snarled. "That's against Facial Regulation 12–BV. Put yourself on report, plebe."

"Yes, sir," Smithers wailed, and scurried off to turn himself in.

That enjoyable encounter having put him in a good mood, Hardy entered the gym and walked up to Cammy Cheesewell.

"You've got the correct materials?" Beef asked Cammy in a low whisper, his eyes darting from side to side to make sure they weren't being watched.

"Stop looking so sneaky," Cammy whispered. "You're making even *me* suspicious."

"Never mind about that," Beef whispered, shielding his face with his cap so that he wouldn't be noticed. "This is our first chance to make sure they fail. I want everything to go smoothly."

"Don't worry," Cammy whispered. "I've got the itching powder right here in this little jar."

"Ssshhhh!" Beef clamped a hand over her mouth. "Don't call it itching powder out loud. Use the code word."

"Code word?" she asked. But since his hand was over her mouth, it came out, "Mmmph mmmpph?"

"Yes," Beef said, pulling his hand away. "The code word. We don't want to be caught, do we?"

"Uh . . . the code word . . ." Cammy thought hard. "Swordfish?"

"No. That's not it," Beef whispered. "Hurry. Use the code word. The exam is almost starting."

"Uh . . . cornflakes with blueberries?"

"What?" Beef cried. "That's not the code word. That's what you had for breakfast."

"Sorry, Beef," Cammy said, lowering her head. "I just don't remember the code word."

Beef sighed, exasperated. "Okay, okay. I'll tell it to you. The code word is *pitching owder*."

"Pitching owder?"

"Yeah. You see, the first letters are reversed. That way, no one will be able to figure out what we're talking about."

Cammy looked at her dream cadet with renewed admiration. "Beef, you're so brilliant!"

"Don't call me Beef," he warned, glancing around the room, which had grown silent, waiting for the instructor to begin the exam. "Call me by my code name."

"Code name?"

"Yes. Call me by my code name," Beef said impatiently. "You remember it — don't you?"

"Well . . . no," Cammy said, her shoulders slumping. She wanted to impress Beef, but so far, she was striking out. "What's your code name?"

"It's Code," Beef whispered. "Code. See? That's my code name."

His words gave her a tingle that ran down her back. How could one cadet be so outrageously clever?

"And do you remember *your* secret name?" Beef asked expectantly.

"Is it Secret?" she asked, taking a wild guess.

"Yes!" he cried aloud, forgetting his nervousness about being overheard. He gave her a pleased smile.

I think I'm getting good at this, Cammy thought.

She pulled the small brown plastic container from her uniform trouser pocket. "Here it is, Code," she whispered. "I've got the pitching owder."

"Sneeze," he said, looking alarmed.

Sneeze? She didn't remember that secret code word.

"Sneeze?" she asked.

"Sneeze!" he cried, his dark eyes growing wide, his face filling with urgency.

"Sneeze? What do you mean, Beef — I mean, Code? What do you mean?"

"I mean I have to sneeze!" he cried.

"Hold it in. Hold it in," she urged. "Don't draw attention to us!"

Nodding at her wisdom, he clasped two fingers over his nose. Then he sneezed out of his mouth so hard that he did a backward cartwheel.

All eyes turned to the back of the gym to see what all the commotion was.

"Yo, Hardy — do that again!" Hunk called.

The room burst into cheers and applause.

"Don't pay any attention," Beef whispered to Cammy, wiping his nose with a handkerchief. Three and a half wipes. The regulation number.

"I don't think they noticed, do you?"

"No, I don't think so," Cammy said, thinking about how handsome he looked when he covered his nose and sneezed out of his mouth.

"So you've got the pitching owder?" Beef asked, returning to business.

"Yes," Cammy whispered.

"Is it good and strong?"

"Well . . . I didn't test it out," Cammy said. "But it's the stuff that's used to torture spies. It should be pretty powerful. It's supposed to start itching as soon as it touches human skin."

"Great!" Beef cried, rubbing his hands together the way people always rub their hands together in the movies. "Okay. The exam is about to start. Let's go over Plan 412."

"Right," Cammy said, holding the small jar tightly in her hand. "Plan 412 . . . uh . . . what's Plan 412 again?"

"It's the plan that comes right after Plan 411," Beef explained patiently.

"Oh, yes. Of course. I stand next to one of the four Space Cadets. When the exam begins and we have to stand at attention for an hour, I raise the jar behind his back, hold it up, and pour some pitching owder down the back of his neck."

"Yes. That's Plan 412," Cadet Hardy said with great seriousness. "When one of the Space Cadets starts howling and scratching and jumping around like an idiot, his three companions will break attention to come to his rescue — and all four will flunk the exam."

"It's a perfect plan," Cadet Cheesewell whispered, with true admiration flaring in her emerald eyes.

"Ssshhh. Don't say *'perfect plan'* out loud," Beef warned. "Reverse the first letters so no one will understand."

"Yes, of course," Cammy whispered, glancing nervously about the vast gym. "It's a perfect plan."

"That's better," Beef said. "Now go to work. Good luck, Secret."

"Thanks, Code," she replied, and she made her way through the lines of cadets, the small brown container wrapped tightly in her hand.

A few minutes later, a lanky lieutenant strode to the front of the room and shouted for quiet. He announced that he was Lieutenant Loafish, the exam proctor, and quickly explained the rules of the exam, his shouted words echoing off the tile walls in a jumble of sound so that not a single word could be understood by anyone.

But no one really had to hear Lieutenant Loafish's explanation. They knew that what they had to do was to stand at full attention for an hour to show that they had discipline.

"Piece of cake," Hunk muttered with a grin.

"Cake? Where? Where?!" Rip cried.

"Sssshhhh!" Shaky warned, holding a trembling finger to his lips to warn Rip. Shaky's knees were knocking together so hard, he looked like he was dancing the Charleston.

Andy beeped and gave the time.

"Atten-*shun*!" Lieutenant Loafish screamed.

And with that cry, the vast gym grew silent, and three hundred gold-and-gray-uniformed cadets sprung to attention, their eyes straight forward, their backs stiff and upright, their arms straight down at their sides.

Except for one cadet, Cammy Cheesewell, who, eyes rigidly to the front, casually, slowly, sneakily raised the hand containing the small bottle of itching powder.

Here goes, she thought.

Here goes Plan 411. Or was it 412?

It cannot fail.

No way it can fail . . .

Making certain that Lieutenant Loafish at the front of the room wasn't watching, she held the open bottle, turned it ever so slightly, and poured a good teaspoonful of itching powder onto the back of the neck of the Space Cadet standing beside her.

To be precise, she poured it onto the neck of Andy.

She then carefully stuffed the bottle into the trouser pocket of her uniform, and stood at perfect, straight attention, waiting for the itching powder to have its immediate effect.

She waited five seconds.

Then five more seconds.

To her surprise, the cadet remained at rigid attention.

Impossible, Cammy Cheesewell declared silently to herself. The itching powder was supposed to work immediately upon contact with human skin.

Did I slip up? she wondered.

Did I pour the powder onto his shirt collar and miss his skin?

Glancing up to the front of the room to make sure Lieutenant Loafish wasn't looking at her, she quickly reached into her trouser pocket, wrapped her hand around the small container, and removed it.

Lieutenant Loafish was walking in front of the rows of cadets, as if doing an inspection tour. He was still on the front row, miles away from her.

Cammy glanced at Cadet Hardy beside her to the right. He stood as straight as a broomstick, not even appearing to breathe.

What a hero, Cammy thought. I can't fail him now.

She took a deep breath, raised the small bottle, and poured another good helping of the white itching powder onto the back of Andy's neck.

Still gripping the bottle, she waited for him to start scratching and leaping about.

She waited.

And waited.

I don't believe this, she exclaimed to herself, a heavy feeling in the pit of her stomach.

She was sure she had poured the powder onto the Space Cadet's neck.

So why wasn't he screaming in agony, slapping at his skin, scratching, jumping, crying? Why wasn't he flunking the exam and causing his buddies to flunk, too?

But Andy remained at perfect attention.

I must have brought the wrong powder, Cammy thought.

Somehow I brought the wrong powder.

This isn't itching powder. It must be talcum powder or bath powder or something equally useless.

I have failed.

She stifled a sob.

Lieutenant Loafish was still several rows in front of her. Cammy glanced at Beef Hardy beside her. "It isn't pitching owder," she whispered, still clutching the half-empty bottle at her side.

"What?" he whispered back without moving his lips, his eyes straight ahead.

"It isn't pitching owder," she repeated through her teeth. "I brought the wrong owder."

"What?" he repeated. She could tell that he was stunned, even though not a single muscle twitched.

"The owder doesn't work," she whispered. "Look."

She raised her hand and poured some of it on the back of Beef Hardy's neck to show him.

Beef didn't react.

For at least two seconds.

Then he let out an ear-splitting whoop. "Yaaaiiiii!" Both hands began flailing wildly, slapping the back of his neck. His head snapped back and forth as he scratched and screamed, and his legs performed a wild dance that would have looked terrific on *Club MTV*.

As Beef Hardy's hands flew up around his neck, he bumped Cammy Cheesewell's arm. The small bottle went flying into the air, and the remaining powder landed on top of her head.

"YIIIIPES!" was Cammy's loud reaction, or something that sounded like it. She began yelping like a puppy with its tail caught in a door, scratching her head and wildly pulling her hair, while doing a complicated dance very similar to Cadet Hardy's.

No one turned to watch the dancing couple. Everyone else in the room remained at rigid attention.

Except for Lieutenant Loafish. He pointed an accusing finger, first at Beef, then at Cammy, and signaling with the same finger, called, "Out. Both of you — out! You fail!"

Still scratching, the two cadets slumped miserably to the exit.

"I don't know what went wrong," Cadet Cheesewell sobbed, furiously scratching her hair with both hands.

"Maybe we should've tried Plan 413," Cadet Hardy lamented, furiously rubbing his red, swollen neck.

Back in the exam room, Andy beeped loudly and gave the current temperature.

Luckily, Lieutenant Loafish was at the front of the room and didn't hear.

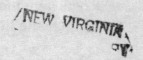

# 8

"YO, HARDY — CAN YOU SHOW ME how to do that dance step?" Hunk yelled across the crowded mess hall. The room erupted in laughter.

Cammy and Beef, sitting across from one another at a table by the door, shoveled their dinner in as quickly as they could in hopes of making a fast escape, the sour taste of defeat in their mouths making it impossible to appreciate their food. The jokes and wisecracks at their expense hadn't stopped ever since the exam had ended and news had gotten around that every cadet had passed except for them.

Now Rip and Hunk were standing up on their table across the room, scratching and leaping about wildly, doing a very good imitation of what Cammy and Beef had looked like just before they had been tossed from the room.

"Pay no attention," Beef said, swallowing hard, his eyes on the floor.

"They're invisible," Cammy said softly, staring into her plate.

"We'll have the last laugh," Beef said bitterly, through clenched teeth.

"What?" Cammy asked. "I can't understand you when you talk through clenched teeth."

"Let's just get out of here," Beef said, pushing away his tray and climbing to his feet.

Across the room, the table had just collapsed beneath Rip's weight, and the four Space Cadets were sprawled on the floor, still scratching as they wildly imitated Beef and Cammy, rolling around in their food, laughing and shouting.

In other words, a typical mess hall dinner.

"Atten-*shun*!" Hunk called, seeing Beef stand up.

This struck everyone in the room funny, and the walls echoed with laughter. Rip stood up and gave a sharp salute, smashing a banana into his forehead.

"Hey — wait just a darned minute, Cadet!" Beef Hardy called angrily, storming over to Rip. "That is *not* a regulation use of a banana! I believe that is a violation of Mess Hall Rule 443–J."

This was the last straw for Beef Hardy. If they wanted to laugh and jeer at him, that was one thing. But he was not about to stand by and watch important food regulations be disobeyed.

"Huh?" Hunk cried with his usual quickness.

"L-leave us alone," Shaky insisted, trying to back away, which wasn't easy since he was already against the wall.

Hardy's fist shot out and caught Shaky on the nose. Shaky cried out in pain.

"Oops. My hand slipped," Hardy said, snickering.

Andy beeped and said, "You leave my friend alone."

Once again, Hardy's fist shot out, this time landing hard in the middle of Andy's face. Andy's nose went flying across the room.

"Wow!" Cammy Cheesewell cried admiringly.

"Guess I don't know my own strength," Hardy boasted gleefully. "Pick up that nose, hotshot, or I'll report you for littering."

As Andy scurried to retrieve his nose, Rip and Hunk closed in on the grinning bully. "Why don't you pick on someone your own size?" Hunk said menacingly.

"Yeah," said Rip, looming over Beef.

This time, both of Hardy's fists shot out. There was a loud popping noise as both fists hit their marks. Rip and Hunk staggered backward, holding their bleeding noses.

With all four Space Cadets moaning and holding their noses, Beef turned sharply and led Cammy triumphantly out of the mess hall.

"That was so awful!" Cammy cried.

"I'm sorry I had to resort to violence," said

Beef, straightening his uniform shirt cuffs. "But they were breaking food regulations."

"Did you hurt your hands?" Cammy asked, taking Beef's hands in hers and rubbing them soothingly.

"I think I got a bad hangnail," Beef said, pouting. He recovered quickly. "But it's all in the line of duty."

"That was terrible how they were laughing at us," Cammy said, still rubbing his hands.

"I think they were laughing more at you than me," Beef said.

It was hard for him to imagine that he would be the object of scorn. After all, he was the top cadet in the class. Destined to finish ahead of everyone — maybe even ahead of himself!

Cammy rubbed his hands tenderly, soothingly, until she had rubbed most of the skin off.

Holding hands with Cammy made him think of Debby Dorque. His one true love.

Sure enough, Debbie had come hurrying up with her camcorder after he and Cammy failed the exam, and asked the two of them to recreate their wild dance for the class video yearbook.

How humiliating. How embarrassing.

Of course he had gone along with it. He had forced Cammy to join him there in the hallway, scratching and dancing the way they had during the exam while Debby taped it all. He just couldn't say no to Debby Dorque.

No way he could say no to her, even with Cammy begging him not to make her dance.

Debby laughed at me, too, Beef thought with almost unbearable sadness.

She laughed until she had tears in her eyes and she had to put down the camcorder.

Don't you realize that I'm going through all this torment, all this pain, for you, Debby? he thought, blowing on his sore hands.

After all, once the Space Cadets had flunked out, Debby would forget about that punk Hunk.

Then she would realize that she belonged with Beef . . .

"Does Commander Dorque know that we failed him?" Cammy asked, as they began to walk toward the study halls.

"It's pronounced Dor-*kay*," Beef corrected her.

"Well, does he know?" Cammy insisted shrilly.

"I have to report to him later," Beef said glumly. "But let's not dwell on one mistake," he added quickly. "Tomorrow is the written exam on Colonial Space Settlements. Maybe the Space Cadets can pass a standing-up test. But there's no way they're going to pass a sitting-down test."

"What do you mean?" Cammy asked, following him down the endless, twisting corridors toward the dormitory area.

"I'm not sure," Beef admitted.

He's so good-looking when he's confused, Cammy thought with a sigh.

* * *

Commander Dorque was pacing back and forth in his office, his thoughts dark and troubled, when his daughter Debby burst in. "What are you doing in here?" he greeted his daughter warmly.

She set down her camcorder on a chair and came over to give him a hug. "Why so glum, Commander Daddy?"

"I'm glum, that's all," he replied. He didn't want to share his problems with her. She wouldn't understand.

"I passed the Discipline Exam this morning," she told him, plopping down in his big, leather desk chair.

"So I heard," he said, sighing. And I heard that those four idiots passed, too, he thought, sighing again.

And how will I retire if they continue to pass their exams?

"I don't like to see you looking like this," Debby said, playing with the letter-opener on the desk.

"I have things on my mind," the headmaster said. And then he blurted out, "I'm thinking of retiring." He hadn't meant to tell her. The thought just escaped from him like air out of a balloon.

His words caught his daughter by surprise. "What?" She dropped the heavy letter-opener, making a three-inch gash on the desktop.

"Just thinking about it. If things go right, I think I might do it."

If things go right. Translation: If the Space Cadets flunk out.

"Oh, Daddy, you're just depressed," Debby said, giving him a reassuring smile. "Know what you need? You need a big slice of Miss Flan's cherry-rhubarb pie. Why don't you go to the kitchen and steal yourself a nice piece?"

Commander Dorque stopped short. His mouth dropped open, and he stared at his daughter in surprise. "I've . . . uh . . . given up cherry-rhubarb pie," he stammered.

Well, it was true. In a way.

He had just come from a talk with Miss Flan. And what an emotional, unsettling talk it had been.

The Commander had poured out his heart to the woman. He had told her everything — of his undying love for her pies, of his desire to make her his bride so they could retire together and she could bake him pies for the rest of their lives.

It was the most romantic speech he had ever given.

Her reply had been a bit disappointing. "I could never marry a thief," she'd said.

He had expected something a little warmer, a little more promising.

"You're a fat little thief," she had added, her round face as hard as stone.

Thus putting an end to his dreams of endless cherry-rhubarb pies.

"You look so forlorn. So miserable. I just hate to see you looking like this," Debby said.

"Then leave my office and you won't have to see me," he said with fatherly warmth.

She bent down and kissed him on top of his bald head. "Okay, okay. I've got to go study, anyway. Just let me put my camcorder away, and I'll be out of here."

Debby picked up the camcorder and carried it into the walk-in supply closet on the other side of the office. She had placed it on the shelf and was just about to come out of the closet when she heard the office door open and someone come in.

Peering out through the half-open closet door, she saw that it was Cadet Beef Hardy. She ducked out of sight and watched him give a spectacular salute that nearly sent him sprawling to his knees. Then he began to talk to her father.

"Cadet Cheesewell and I failed," Hardy was saying. "We tried to get those four to flunk, but our plan didn't work. But don't worry, sir. There's no way they're going to pass this term. We'll get them to flunk tomorrow."

Very interesting, thought Debby, raising the camcorder to her eye. So Hardy and Cheesewell and my father are cooking up a little plot against Hunk and his friends. No *wonder* Daddy looked so nervous when I came in. And now he's forgotten I'm here.

Hidden by the closet door, Debby held her breath, listening in frozen silence to the rest of the conversation. When it had ended, she watched Cadet Hardy knock himself to the floor with an enthusiastic salute, pick himself up, and leave. A few seconds later, her father left, too.

Well, well, well, thought Debby.

Well, well, well, well, well.

Well, well, well, well, well, well, well, well, well.

I'd better get out of this closet and go think about what to do, she decided. And, after a few more wells, she put away the camcorder, stepped out of the closet, locked the door behind her, and headed to her room.

# 9

INSIDE THEIR DORM ROOM, the four Space Cadets
were tending to their noses. Andy had managed
to reattach his with the help of some Krazy Glue.
The other three were dabbing at theirs with cold
compresses, waiting for the bleeding to stop.

A short while later, Rip put down his after-
dinner ham sandwich and picked up a letter he
had just received by rocketmail. "It's from my
kid brother," Rip said proudly. "Listen to this."

Struggling to make out the handwriting, he
proceeded to read the letter to his three buddies:

*Dear Rip,*
*How are things at the Space Academy? I hope you*
*are fine.*
*Things are pretty good here at home. Mom gave up*
*worming and is making a pretty good living selling*
*cups of dirt. You'd be surprised at the demand for dirt*
*cups. We keep having to go out and buy more cups so*
*Mom can fill them.*

*Dad is still clucking like a chicken, but we're kinda getting used to it. It's when he bends down and pecks around on the gravel drive that it's a little hard to take.*

*Mom says if she sells two hundred more dirt cups, we'll be able to take Dad to a real doctor, and not just Mr. Barnes, who thinks he's a doctor but is really a barber who isn't allowed to handle sharp instruments.*

*I'm going back to school as soon as my suspension is over, and this time I'm going to do as good as you did, Rip. Which means it should only take me seven or eight years to graduate high school, if I only flunk each grade once.*

*We're all real proud of you, big brother. Thanks for sending the real, official space suit that you stole from the Academy warehouse. It fits Dad really well, and makes him look really nice when he's out back pecking around in the gravel.*

*Mom is real proud of you, too, Rip. She's going to send you a cup of dirt when she gets the chance.*

*Good luck on your exams, bro. We all can't wait to see what you can steal for us when you're a real Space Patrolman.*

*Love,*
*Flathead*

"Isn't that a sweet letter?" Rip asked, genuinely touched.

"Let me see that," Hunk said, grabbing the letter from Rip's hand. Hunk stared at the letter for a few seconds. "Hey — how'd your brother get the name Flathead?" he asked.

"It's an old family name," Rip replied.

"I love the letters from your brother," Andy said. "They make me feel homesick."

"Really?" Rip asked. "Where's your home?"

"An electronics factory on Mercury," Andy replied.

"My nose hurts," Shaky said. "That Beef Hardy is a horrible bully."

"Forget about him," Hunk said, admiring his profile in a hand mirror. Once the swelling went down, his face would be as fabulous as ever, he determined. "We can't worry about him now. We've got to study, guys. We all really want to be in the Space Patrol, right?"

"Right," the others agreed.

"My brother is counting on me," Rip said.

"A lot of people are counting on us. If we work together, we'll make it," Hunk said with real emotion.

The four comrades put their arms around each other's shoulders and hugged each other. Unfortunately, Rip hugged with a little too much enthusiasm, and Andy's nose popped off again.

"No problem," Andy said. "Start studying without me. I'll have the nasal unit back on in a jiffy."

But without his nose, no one could understand a word he said.

*   *   *

While this touching conversation was taking place inside the dorm room, Cadets Beef Hardy and Cammy Cheesewell were searching the halls, looking for that very room. "I think that's their door, the one that says MEN on it," Beef said.

"Isn't that the men's rest room?" Cammy asked.

"No. I think they painted the word on the door. You know, just to be cute."

At that moment, Debby Dorque, carrying a pile of textbooks instead of her usual camcorder, came around the corner. "Hiya," she said absently.

"Debby!" Beef cried. "Can I carry those for you?"

"No, thanks. I'm already carrying them," Debby said coldly.

Cammy nudged Beef hard in the ribs. "We have a mission — remember?" she whispered.

Beef's normally emotionless face reddened. "Uh . . . Debby, you wouldn't happen to know where Hunk's room is, would you?" he asked, trying to sound casual.

Debby stopped. She seemed to think for a minute. "Yes," she said finally. "It's on the twentieth floor. Room 2034."

"Thanks a lot," Beef said, with more enthusiasm than was called for. "Perhaps later you and I could meet and discuss room numbers. I know some really interesting ones. Maybe — "

82

But Debby had turned the corner and disappeared.

A few minutes later, Beef and Cammy were standing outside Room 2034, having a whispered planning conversation.

"Why does it smell of bologna in there?" Cammy whispered, sniffing the air.

"They buy these spray cans of artificial bologna fragrance and they spray the smell in," Beef told her. "They like it, I guess."

She crinkled her stubby nose and made a disgusted face. "Gross."

"Yes. Anyone whose room smells like artificial bologna doesn't belong in the Interplanetary Space Patrol," Beef said. He felt like saluting, but restrained himself.

"I agree," Cammy said, giving him an admiring look. "So here is my plan for tomorrow's exam."

"*Your* plan?" Beef was a little taken aback. "I thought I was in charge."

"Oh. Okay." Cammy's face filled with disappointment. "What's *your* plan?"

"I don't have a plan," Beef admitted. "Why don't we try *your* plan?"

Cammy's creamy white face brightened again. "Okay. Good idea. I call my plan Plan Number 114."

"No. Call it Z–12," Beef whispered.

"You're so good at this," she said, meaning it as a sincere compliment.

"Thank you," Beef said stiffly. She's a smart girl, he thought. A very smart girl. "So let's hear Plan Z–12."

"Well, we make a lot of funny noises," Cammy said. She studied his face to see if he liked the idea.

His handsome, rugged-featured face showed only bewilderment. "Funny noises? That's Plan Z–12?"

She nodded her head yes.

"How long do we make the funny noises?" Beef asked, rubbing his perfect chin thoughtfully, studying his own reflection in her green eyes.

"All night," Cammy answered. She realized she felt terribly nervous. Maybe, maybe, she thought, if he really likes my plan, he'll like me, too.

"We make funny noises all night?" Beef repeated, still confused. "That's Plan Z–12?"

"Yes. That's my plan," Cammy said, giving him a confident smile.

He thought about it. "I like it," he said finally.

"You do?? Really??" she cried.

He muffled her mouth with his hand. They were standing right outside the Space Cadets' door, after all.

"I think it shows a lot of promise," Beef said. "I *do* have a few very minor questions, however."

"Oh, really?" Cammy asked. "Like what?"

"Well . . . like *why* do we make funny noises all night?"

The question seemed to catch her by surprise. She leaned her back against the corridor wall and closed her eyes. "Because they'll be studying all night for the Colonial Space Settlement exam, right?"

"Right," Beef said.

"But if we make funny noises outside their door and outside their window, they'll be distracted. They'll wonder what the noises are, and they won't be able to study. See?"

Beef nodded thoughtfully.

"They'll spend the whole night trying to track down the funny noises, and they won't get any studying done. And then in the morning, they'll all flunk the test."

"Brilliant!" Beef cried. "Absolutely brilliant!"

Cammy muffled his mouth with her hand.

"Mmmmpph mmmpph mmmmpph," he said.

She took her hand away. "What did you say?"

"Absolutely brilliant!"

She could feel herself blushing. She was so happy, she felt like throwing her arms around his perfectly pressed uniform.

"What kind of funny noises?" he asked, interrupting her thoughts.

"You know," she said.

"I do?"

"Yeah. Just funny noises."

"You mean like this?" Beef asked. He removed his uniform jacket, unbuttoned his uniform shirt, put his hand in his armpit, and cranked his arm, making several loud pfffffftt sounds.

Just as he did this, two cadets came walking past. "Hardy sure knows how to impress a girl," one said to the other. They burst out laughing as they turned a corner.

"What's their problem?" Beef asked, his hand still in his armpit.

"They're just jealous," Cammy said, smiling at him tenderly. "But that isn't the kind of funny sound I meant."

Beef looked disappointed. He removed his hand, resisted the temptation to smell his fingers, and started to button up his shirt.

"I meant like animal sounds," Cammy explained. "Like this." She started to hoot like an owl. "Hoo hoo. Hoo hoooo."

"Oh. That's good. That's good," Beef said enthusiastically. "That's a cat, right? Here. Let me try one." He scrunched up his handsome face and began cheeping like a bird. "Cheep cheep. Cheeep cheeeep."

Just as he was really getting into it, the same two cadets came walking past again, this time heading the other way. "Hardy really knows how to show a girl a good time," one of them said, and they broke up in hysterics again.

"That was very good," Cammy said.

"How about this one?" Beef cried. He began mooing like a cow.

"That's awesome," Cammy said, truly impressed.

"Well, it's a familiar sound. My family used to own a herd of cows," Beef said modestly.

"You had a dairy farm?"

"Dairy farm? What do you mean?" Beef asked, bewildered.

"You know. The herd of cows. Did you own them for their milk?" Cammy asked.

"Milk? You can get milk from cows?" Beef looked positively astonished. "No one told us." he said, slapping his forehead. "No *wonder* Mom and Dad couldn't make a living. We kept the cows for their *fur*!"

"Let's get back to Plan Z–12," Cammy suggested. "There's a walkway right outside the Space Cadets' dorm window. One of us can get out on the walkway and make funny noises out there. And one of us can stay here by the door and make funny noises."

"Brilliant!" Beef Hardy said again. He stifled another urge to salute. "That'll really confuse them."

"Yes, that's the idea," Cammy said. "When they look out the window, we'll just duck around the corner. When they open the door, we can hide behind that storage crate over there," she said, pointing to it. "That way we can keep them guessing all night. They won't have a second to study!"

"It's perfect," Beef said enthusiastically.

"Why don't you take the walkway outside the window, and I'll take the door?" Cammy suggested, glancing at her watch.

Beef thought it over. "No," he said, shaking his head. "Why don't you take the door, and I'll take the walkway?"

"Okay," Cammy agreed. "If you like that better."

"No. I changed my mind. You had it right the first time," Beef said. "I'll take the walkway and you take the door."

"Okay. Sounds good," Cammy agreed. "Good luck. See you in the morning."

"Yes, good luck," Beef said seriously, shaking her hand. He started to walk away, but stopped and came back. "I'm sorry. Let me get this straight. Do I take the walkway and you take the door, or do you take the door and I take the walkway?"

"I take the door, and you take the walkway," Cammy said patiently. "Unless you want it the other way around."

"No, no. That's fine," Beef said, thinking it over. He stepped close to her. "Cammy," he said softly, "there's just one other thing I wanted to ask you."

"Yes?" she whispered expectantly, leaning close to him.

He hesitated.

"Go on," she whispered. "What is it, Beef?"

"Which do you like better — my cow or my canary?"

It was cold out on the ledge, but Cadet Hardy didn't mind. He had a mission to perform.

The strong, gusting winds made him lean against the building for support. He was at least twenty stories up in the air.

"I don't mind dying while on duty," he told himself. But he really didn't want to die while mooing like a cow on a window ledge.

He wanted to button his uniform jacket to the top. But that was against the dress code regulations, which called for three buttons only, except for formal occasions or space wars.

A light rain began to fall, a misty drizzle that turned into a steady, cold downpour.

"Moooooo," he called at the dark window. The shades were drawn. He couldn't see inside. But he knew his mooing must be driving the four Space Cadets crazy, keeping them from studying a word.

He wondered how Cammy was doing at the doorway. He wondered if she was doing her cat sounds or her barking seal. He wondered how her throat was holding out. His was getting pretty sore.

Maybe he should start cheeping like a canary for a while and save his throat. Then he could get back to mooing in the early morning hours when it really counted.

He stifled a yawn and started to cheep.

If only it weren't so cold and wet. Maybe he should go inside and ask Cammy to trade places with him for a while.

No. An Interplanetary Space Patrolman on a serious mission would never do that.

He had a sudden impulse to salute. But he knew it would knock him off the ledge, so he stifled the urge.

"Cheep cheeep cheeeep!"

He giggled, thinking of the confusion he must be causing on the other side of the window. He coughed. His throat was really sore. Maybe he'd better switch to a new animal. How about a pig? he thought. Excellent. Now how do pigs go? He couldn't remember. His parents had owned only cows.

"Cheeep cheeep cheeep." He decided to stick with what he knew.

The rain stopped, but the wind continued to roar. Commander Dorque will be proud, Beef thought. And Debby. Debby would be proud of him, too. Some day.

The hours dragged by. He clucked like a chicken for a while, just for variety.

This plan has to work, he thought, as a purple sun began to rise through the parting clouds. There's no way those four clowns are getting any studying done in there. Not with Cammy and me bombarding them with these sounds.

He was soaked to the skin and his throat throbbed with pain. But he knew it would be worth it when the Space Cadets failed their written exam.

The sun was a red globe now, rising higher into the morning sky. He glanced at his watch. Time to get changed and go in for breakfast.

Hooray!

He straightened up, took a deep breath and stretched, glad the long night was over. Then he turned away from the window, took two steps, and fell off the ledge.

# 10

By the time Beef Hardy got to the mess hall for breakfast, he had a hacking cough and his throat was so sore, he couldn't speak.

Falling off the ledge hadn't turned out as badly as it might have. Luckily, there was a wider ledge on the floor just below, and so he had fallen less than six feet.

A piece of cake. All in the line of duty.

He had fallen with a *thud*, but if he was hurt by the fall, he was too wet and too exhausted to notice.

When he returned to his room and gazed at himself in his trusty dresser mirror, he was appalled by what he saw. His normally lustrous hair was dull and plastered against his head, which violated Grooming Rule 12–CC. His eyes were red-rimmed and bloodshot, which violated Hygiene Rule 879–K. Even a scalding hot shower couldn't return the color to his pallid cheeks.

"I'm a mess," he croaked. "I'm not regulation."

But he didn't care. Not if it meant success for mission Z–12.

He staggered down to the mess hall, so tired he forgot to punch a plebe in the face. He managed to locate Cammy sipping a cup of orange juice at their usual table.

"How are you?" he tried to say. His mouth moved, but no sounds came out. He had lost his voice entirely.

"Croak croak," Cammy replied.

"You can stop the funny animal sounds," he said in a soft whisper. "It's morning now."

"Croak croak," Cammy replied. She pointed to her throat. Beef quickly caught on. Her throat was so sore, she couldn't talk. She could only croak.

She smiled at him. He smiled back. Her head hit the table as she fell asleep.

He shook her hard, finally managing to wake her. "We have to go take the Colonial Space Settlement exam," he reminded her.

"Croak?" She couldn't hear him.

"The exam," he whispered.

"Croak?"

Their conversation was interrupted by the sight of Hunk, Rip, Shaky, and Andy bounding energetically into the mess hall. To Beef's utter dismay, all four of them looked happy, bright-eyed, and well rested. They were laughing loudly despite the early hour, and began enthusiastically tossing breakfast rolls at each other.

"Hey — look at them," Beef whispered to Cammy.

"Croak croak?"

"They don't look tired. But they've *gotta* be! They must be faking it," Beef whispered.

"Croak?" Cammy asked. She really couldn't hear Beef at all.

Her head hit the table as she fell asleep again. Again, Beef revived her by shaking her shoulders.

"I'm going over and talk to them," Beef mouthed.

"Croak?" Cammy replied.

So exhausted he could barely see straight, Beef stumbled over to Hunk and his three buddies. Seeing him approach, all four Space Cadets immediately raised their hands to cover their noses.

"Aren't you guys — tired?" Beef managed to ask.

"What? Speak up, Hardy," Hunk said, unable to hear.

"Croak croak?" Cammy called from across the room.

"Aren't you tired after last night?" Beef asked.

Hunk looked confused. "Last night? We all went to bed early," he told Beef. "Big exam today, you know. We studied for a while. Then we hit the sack. We wanted to be rested for it."

"Exam? What exam? I forget," Shaky said. He was trembling and shaking the table so hard, the soft-boiled egg on his plate turned into a scrambled egg.

"You mean — you slept?" Beef asked in disbelief.

"We all slept like babies," Hunk told him.

"Like babies," Andy repeated. "Ha . . . ha . . . ho . . ."

"But — but — didn't you hear any funny noises?" Beef asked, hardly able to mouth the words.

Hunk thought about it. "No . . . no funny noises. Just Rip snoring. But we hear that every night."

"I don't snore," Rip insisted angrily. "I'm just a loud breather." He had a giant-sized box of cornflakes in front of him. He poured a container of milk into the box and began wolfing down the cereal right from the box.

"Come to think of it . . ." Hunk said, thinking hard.

"Yes? Yes?" Beef whispered eagerly.

"I did hear a loud crash outside our window early this morning. It woke me up for a few seconds."

"I heard it, too," Shaky said. "It scared me. Sounded like someone falling onto the ledge or something. It took me nearly thirty seconds to fall back asleep."

95

"Ha . . . ha . . . hee . . . hee . . ." said Andy, and he beeped loudly. "Pardon me," he added, holding his hand over his mouth.

Beef didn't like what he was hearing. He was beginning to think there may have been an important flaw in Plan Z–12. "You heard something fall onto your ledge this morning, huh?" he asked, struggling to make himself heard. "Your room is on the twentieth floor, right? Room 2034?"

"Huh-uh, man," Hunk shook his head. "We're on nineteen. Room 1934."

Beef let out a high-pitched *eek* and sank to his knees, his eyes spinning in his head.

He and Cammy had serenaded the wrong room. After staying up all night in the rain, mooing into the wrong window, he had fallen down to the right window.

How could Debby Dorque, his one true love, have made such a hideous mistake?

Rip, still chewing cornflakes, helped Beef to his feet. "You okay, man?"

"You look terrible," Shaky told him.

"Better get your gear displacements checked," Andy advised.

"Yo — let's go, guys," Hunk said, standing up. "Time for the exam."

"Exam? What exam?" Shaky asked.

Beef didn't hear them. His brain was exploding. The whole room was spinning. Somehow he

96

managed to stagger back to Cammy, who was waiting at the table across the room.

"Croak croak croak?" she asked eagerly as he stood uncertainly across from her.

"Fine," he said. "Just fine." He didn't have the heart to tell her.

Yawning loudly, they helped each other into the exam room and took their assigned desks. Less than two minutes after the exam started, both Beef and Cammy put their heads down on their desks to take a little rest.

It wasn't until the bell rang an hour later, startling them awake, that they realized they had slept through the entire exam.

# 11

COMMANDER DORQUE LEANED FORWARD over his desk and took a big bite out of his club sandwich. He had ordered the club sandwich without the lettuce, without the tomato, without the turkey, and without the bacon.

He chewed for a while, then made a face. "Kind of dry." Why was it so hard to get a good club sandwich these days?

Frowning, the headmaster put down the two slices of toast and picked up the long sheets of computer printout containing the morning test scores.

To his dismay, he read for the twentieth time — still not believing it — that Cadets Beef Hardy and Camembert Cheesewell had scored perfect zeros on their Colonial Space Settlements exam.

The Commander burped uncomfortably and took another bite of his empty club sandwich as he contemplated this unfortunate news. Hardy and Cheesewell were two top Space Patrol candidates. They had never scored below a ninety-seven before. And now they had failed their first two exams.

This unsettling news was made better only by the fact that all four Space Cadets had also flunked the exam. A smile crossed Commander Dorque's pudgy face as he added up their four test scores. Putting all four test scores together, the Space Cadets had managed to score a ten.

Not bad, not bad, the Commander thought, folding his arms behind his head and leaning back in his tall, leather desk chair. He closed his eyes and dreamily thought of his retirement.

Soon they will flunk, and I will be away, he thought. Away from the Space Academy. Away from the Space Cadets, from *all* the cadets. Off on a quiet planet somewhere.

If only his plans for the cherry-rhubarb pies had worked out. Then his retirement would be complete bliss.

His stomach rumbled so violently, he slid off the chair and hit the floor with a loud *plop*.

Someone is deliberately oiling my chair, he thought, pulling himself up slowly to his feet. He climbed back up onto the seat and pulled the seat belt over his bulging stomach.

Picking up the computer printout again, he

decided to concentrate on something more pleasant — like the Space Cadets flunking their final two exams.

Andy beeped and gave the time. "Time to study for the next exam," he announced.

"What is the next exam?" Shaky asked. "I forget." He had been trying for nearly half an hour to thread a needle so he could sew a tear in Rip's uniform. His hands were shaking so hard, he didn't realize that he'd dropped the needle and the thread ten minutes ago.

"Hey — can one of you guys help me do this?" Shaky asked finally.

"Sure," Andy replied. He watched Shaky for a minute. Then he began shaking his hands just like Shaky. A perfect imitation. "Is this helping?"

"Never mind," Shaky said, giving up. "What's the next exam?"

"It's Weapon Skills," Hunk said, looking at himself in the mirror as he finished shaving. Not bad, he thought. Only three bleeding cuts.

"Yes, Weapon Skills," Shaky said, suddenly remembering. "That's guns and stuff, right?"

Rip was sitting on the edge of the bed, putting on his shoes and socks. "Hey — I need a sock," he exclaimed, holding up only one of a pair.

"What did you say?" Hunk asked, turning eagerly away from the mirror.

"I need a sock!" Rip repeated.

"Okay," Hunk said. He walked over and gave Rip a playful sock on the chest.

"Hey!" Rip jumped to his feet. "I said I needed a sock — not a sock!"

"No problem, man," Hunk said, and socked him again.

"Ha . . . ha . . . ho . . . ho," said Andy. "I need a sock."

"Okay," Rip said, and socked Andy in the chest. Andy made a funny *boinging* noise. His chest seemed to cave in, then bounced right back.

"Shaky — do you need a sock?" Hunk asked.

Shaky looked nervously down at his ankles. "No, I don't think so. Thanks."

Hunk socked him anyway.

Then Rip socked Hunk, Shaky socked Andy, Andy beeped and socked Shaky, Hunk socked Rip, Shaky socked Hunk, Rip socked Andy, Hunk socked Shaky, Andy socked Rip, and Rip socked Andy and Shaky.

All four Space Cadets were socking away when the door opened and Debby Dorque looked in. "Hunk," she cried, "what are you doing?"

"Uh . . . we're studying," he replied.

# 12

A FEW MINUTES BEFORE the Weapon Skills exam
was about to be held in the target room, Cammy
Cheesewell met Beef Hardy out in the corridor.
Cammy's voice hadn't returned; she was still
croaking like a bullfrog. Beef had the worst cold
of his life.

As they tried to plot their next strategy, their
conversation sounded something like this:

"Croak croak croak?"

"AH-CHOO!"

"Croak croak?"

"Dub blubb blubbb AH-CHOOOO?"

"Croak. Croak croak. Croak."

"AH-CHOOO! Blub blub dub blub. Sniff sniff."

"Croak?"

"Sniff sniff sniff sniff. Blub blub."

"Croak croak!"

"I don't know."

"Croak croak croak?"

"AH-CHOOOO!"

"Croak croak. Please cover your nose."

"AH-CHOOO!"

"Not with my uniform sleeve!"

"Sorry." Beef apologized. "I think I have a temperature," he moaned. "It feels like at least a hundred and six."

"Is that a record?" Cammy croaked. "Oh, Beef, I'm so proud of you. I knew you could get better than a hundred if you tried!"

He sneezed in reply, grabbing her uniform sleeve as a handkerchief. "Are you okay, Cammy? You look as bad as I feel."

"Thank you," she said uncertainly. She croaked a further reply, but Beef couldn't understand a word of it.

"Well, this isn't the time to think about ourselves," Beef said, turning serious. He wanted to salute, but he knew it would only make him sneeze.

"The Weapon Skills exam is about to begin," Cammy said, taking a few steps back and holding her sleeves behind her in case he did sneeze again. "What are we going to do to make sure the Space Cadets flunk?"

"No problem," Beef said. He leaned close so he could whisper confidentially, and sneezed into her ear.

He's so adorable when he sneezes like that,

Cammy thought, vigorously shaking her head.

"I've taken care of everything," Beef whispered.

"How?" she croaked.

"Well, first I checked the exam list. Hunk and his three buddies are scheduled to go first for target practice. You and I are scheduled to shoot right after them."

Cammy croaked a reply. Beef had no idea what she had said, so he continued explaining his plan.

"So, since they're going first, I fixed their phaser guns for them."

"You what?" Cammy asked.

"I have a friend in the weapons supply room. He and I go outside and shoot innocent creatures sometimes on weekends."

"That's nice," Cammy said.

"He gave me a key, and I sneaked into the gun supply room late last night. I found the four phaser guns that will be used for the exam this morning. And I put a little explosive charge in each."

"You mean — "

"I mean when the four morons fire their phaser guns, the guns will blow their heads off," Beef said, his nose dripping into the broad smile that had formed on his feverishly red face. "And they'll automatically flunk the exam."

"Brilliant!" Cammy exclaimed.

"AH-CHOOOO!" Beef replied.

"Croak croak croak."

"Sniff sniff sniff."

"Croak croak. Urp. Excuse me."

"And as they carry the Space Cadets off in disgrace," Beef said, grinning, "you and I will take up our weapons and show the examiner how real cadets shoot!"

"Brilliant!" Cammy repeated. "But are you *sure* it's necessary to kill them to make sure they flunk the exam?"

"I didn't say it would kill them," Beef replied impatiently. "Killing them is against Regulation 1–A. I just said it would blow their heads off."

"Huh?" Cammy croaked.

"If blowing their heads off results in their accidental death, that's not against regulations — right?"

"I see," said Cammy admiringly. "You're so smart. You really do know your regulations."

"Not knowing your regulations is against regulations," said Beef earnestly.

Then, arm in arm, sneezing and croaking, they opened the door and entered the target room.

The long, low room was already filled with cadets. They stood in clusters at one end, staring down the narrow target aisles at the human-looking cardboard cutout targets at the other end.

"Attention!" cried the familiar voice of Lieutenant Barney Broadside, the weapons instructor. It was a standard cadet joke that Barney Broadside couldn't hit the broad side of a barn.

Actually, Broadside was nearly as *big* as a barn, and tremendously muscular, so no one had ever dared make that joke to his face.

The cadets eagerly snapped to attention. Broadside lifted a basket containing the four phaser guns to be used in the exam. "I hope you all brought your shooting eyes today," he bellowed. "You need a perfect score to pass my exam."

The instructor called up Hunk, Rip, Andy, and Shaky to go first. They stepped up smartly to the front of the room, formed a line, and stood at rigid attention as Broadside paced back and forth, inspecting them.

Beef glanced knowingly at Cammy beside him. He couldn't wait for those four morons to pull the triggers. He couldn't wait to see the guns blow their heads off. He couldn't wait to see them carried from the target room in disgrace. And he couldn't wait to sneeze.

"AH-CHHOOOO!"

Lieutenant Broadside spun angrily around. "One more outburst like that, and I'll flunk the entire squadron!" he screamed.

Beef took a deep breath and held it.

"Don't blow it," Cammy whispered.

"My nose?"

"No. Don't blow the plan."

"Oh."

Lieutenant Broadside was standing in front of the four Space Cadets, looking them over. "Rip, you're out of uniform," Broadside said sternly.

"I know, sir. I need a sock," Rip replied.

"You need a sock?" Andy asked. He stepped forward and socked Rip in the stomach.

"Hey!" Rip cried. He socked Andy in the shoulder.

Then Hunk socked Rip. Then Rip socked Shaky, Shaky socked himself, Hunk socked Rip, Shaky socked himself again, Andy socked Rip, and Rip socked Andy and Hunk.

Beef and Cammy watched the whole sordid episode gleefully. This is *great,* thought Beef.

"Out! Get out!" Broadside was bellowing at the top of his enormous lungs. "Get out of the target room! All four of you flunk!"

This is *great,* thought Beef.

"Huh? We flunk?" Hunk asked, holding off Andy, who wanted to do some more socking.

"Yes. You flunk," Broadside said, pointing to the door. "After this idiotic display, I'd have to be *crazy* to put a gun in your hands. So you flunk. Get out of here — now!"

This is *great,* thought Beef.

The four Space Cadets glumly slumped out of the target room.

Great, great, *great!*

"Next!" called Lieutenant Broadside. "Cadets Beef Hardy and Camembert Cheesewell!" He held up the pistols as Cammy and Beef stepped to the front.

This is *not* so great! thought Beef.

The guns hadn't been touched. That meant they were still set to explode when the trigger was pulled.

Cammy looked at Beef.

Beef looked at Cammy.

Broadside handed them each a phaser pistol.

"You two are my best target shooters," he said. "Show them all how it's done."

Cammy looked at her gun.

Beef looked at his gun.

Cammy raised her gun toward the target.

Beef raised his gun toward the target.

"Fire at will," said Broadside.

"Who's Will?" Rip called from the side.

"I *told* you guys to get out of here!" Broadside bellowed.

Rip obediently lumbered out of the room.

Cammy looked at her gun. Then at Beef.

Beef stared back at her.

"We — can't," Beef told Lieutenant Broadside, lowering the phaser gun.

"We can't," Cammy agreed.

"What do you *mean* you can't?!" Broadside bellowed.

"We just can't," Beef said.

Cammy croaked the same words.

Beef sneezed loudly.

"Get out of here," Broadside ordered. "You flunk, too!"

"Maybe we could come back to this part of the exam — later?" Cammy asked softly.

"Yeah. We'll take our turn after the next four cadets," Beef suggested eagerly.

"Out!" Broadside bellowed. "You flunked."

Cammy and Beef sadly handed back the phaser guns. Broadside called up the next four cadets and ordered them to begin shooting.

Beef sneezed. My temperature must be at least 108, he thought miserably. The highest score I've gotten all week.

The four phaser guns exploded loudly as Beef and Cammy glumly made their way through the exit. They didn't even turn around to see who had been blown up.

# 13

"IMPOSSIBLE," COMMANDER DORQUE MUTTERED aloud. He ran his eyes over the computer printout one more time. "Impossible," he repeated.

The office was empty and dark except for the narrow cone of light from the desk lamp. Miss Moon had gone home hours ago after a hard day of not knowing how to do anything.

The headmaster rubbed his aching forehead, trying to soothe away his persistent headache. "Impossible," he repeated, his expression troubled.

How could the first ten cadets who took the Weapon Skills exam flunk it?

There was only one word for it, the word the Commander had been repeating over and over to the four walls of his office — *impossible!*

He held the test results under the desk lamp and went over them again in order. "Let's see now . . . maybe I'm not reading this thing correctly."

No. It was just as he had read it the first two dozen times.

First the four Space Cadets flunked.

Well, that was to be expected.

Broadside had tossed them out without even giving them a chance to shoot. Good man, Broadside. He should be given a promotion for that.

But then what happened?

Cheesewell and Hardy, the two best target-shooters in the class, refused to shoot, and they, too, flunked out. And then the next four cadets misfired somehow and nearly blew their own heads off!

Not very impressive.

Not very impressive at all, Dorque thought, rubbing harder at his throbbing headache. He tossed down the test results and began to massage his pink flesh with both hands.

There was only one cure for this headache.

Only one cure for all the troubles of the day.

And the cure sat waiting for him in the pantry outside the kitchen. The cure, of course, being a large helping of Carmella Flan's cherry-rhubarb pie.

Commander Dorque couldn't stop himself. Before he realized it, his feet were taking him out of the office. And now his feet were taking him down the twisting, empty corridor. And now his feet were taking him into the kitchen, and his eyes were searching the dimly lit room, making sure the coast was clear.

It wasn't.

Carmella Flan stood in the dim gray light, watching over her pie pantry.

"Just a surprise kitchen inspection," said the Commander, thinking quickly, drawing himself up to his full height of almost five feet.

"Thief!" Carmella Flan said quietly but firmly. "You're a fat little thief, Commander Dorque."

"It's Dor-*kay*," he insisted, and fled back to his office in fear and disappointment.

"The only exam left is the physical exam," Beef Hardy moaned. He shifted the ice pack on his fevered brow.

"No problem," Cammy Cheesewell croaked. "No problem at all." She went into a coughing fit that could only be stopped by Beef pounding on her back with all his strength.

His strength wasn't terribly impressive. His cold had developed into the flu. He no longer had the strength to sneeze. He could only AH — he couldn't CHOO.

The two ill and exhausted cadets were lying side by side on cots in the infirmary, plotting their final plot to make sure the Space Cadets didn't pass their exams.

"No problem? How can you say it's no problem?" Beef wailed, staring at his reflection in the ceiling light fixture. "I stayed up all night thinking about it." He tried to sit up, but his eyes started to swim in his head, and he lay back down.

He looks so handsome when his eyes swim around like that, Cammy thought.

"I've already taken care of it," she informed him, croaking out the words through her painfully sore and swollen throat.

"Huh?"

The effort of saying "huh" forced Beef to close his eyes and take a short nap. When he awakened, Cammy explained. "I put something in that candy stuff the four of them are always eating," she said. "You know — those fruit stickups."

"Yeah, that's all they eat. Fruit stickups," Beef said. And then he added, "AH — AH — AH — " But he wasn't able to CHOO.

"Well, I stayed up all night, too," Cammy croaked. "I waited by their door all night. Then this morning, when they headed off to breakfast, I sneaked into their dormitory room and injected a chemical into their fruit stickups."

"I hope it isn't a *harmless* chemical," Beef said.

"No. It isn't harmless at all," Cammy said.

This news seemed to cheer Beef considerably. "What will it do to them?" he asked, a little color returning to his cheeks.

"Turn them bright blue," Cammy said, before going into another lengthy coughing fit.

"Huh?"

"The chemical will turn their skin bright blue for twenty-four hours. All four of them will be as blue as baboons."

"As baboons?" Beef asked.

"Well, whatever," Cammy replied impatiently. "They'll be real blue. And there's no way Dr. Dewlittle will let them pass their physical if they're bright blue!"

"Brilliant!" declared Beef. "Absolutely brilliant! Soon, all four of them will be singing the blues!"

"Beef — was that a joke you just made?" Cammy croaked.

"Yes, I believe it was," Beef told her.

They both tried to laugh, but the strain was too much. Instead, they fell into a deep sleep and didn't awaken until it was time for the final exam of the semester — the physical.

# 14

CAMMY CHEESEWELL WAS ONE OF THE FIRST to take the physical exam. Beef Hardy saw her in the waiting room, crowded with cadets, as she left Dr. Dewlittle's office. "Well?" he asked. "How did you AH — AH — AH — ?"

"Croak croak," she replied miserably.

"You failed?" Beef cried, slapping his forehead so hard in surprise that he toppled to the floor and two cadets had to help him to his feet.

"I — I'm just exhausted," Cammy said weakly. "I guess I shouldn't have stayed up all those nights, plotting against you-know-who."

Just as she said this, the waiting-room door swung open, and in walked the four Space Cadets, all of them talking loudly, all of them shoving and tripping each other playfully, all of them as blue as baboons.

None of the cadets in the crowded waiting room said a word to them about their new skin color. No one even had the nerve to say: "That's funny — you don't look *blue-ish*!"

That's because the other cadets were convinced that Hunk and his pals had done this to themselves as some sort of dumb practical joke — or that they had caught some kind of weird disease.

Beef saw them enter, and a pleased smile crossed his face. Maybe poor Cammy had failed her physical. But there was *no way* these four clowns were going to pass.

Which meant that his mission had been a success, and Commander Dorque would be pleased.

Beef wanted to say more to Cammy, to comfort her in some way. But she had already fled back to her room. After several minutes, during which he stared happily across the waiting room at the four blue-skinned Space Cadets, Beef's name was called by the nurse, and he hurried into Dr. Dewlittle's office for his exam.

"Cadet Hardy, you look terrible," was the doctor's greeting.

Beef leaned against the door frame for support. No one had ever said that to him before in his life.

"AH — AH — AH — " he informed the doctor.

The doctor's round, spectacled face filled with concern. "No CHOO?" he asked. "Lie down here, young man. Let me examine you."

He began the exam, taking Beef's temperature and blood pressure, listening to his chest with a stethoscope, tsk-tsking the whole while.

"I've been under a lot of pressure lately," Beef explained without being asked. And then he added, "AH — AH — AH — "

"Muscle tone is nonexistent," the doctor frowned. He looked into Beef's eyes.

"I guess I look a little green today," Beef said quietly.

"Green?" Dr. Dewlittle stared at him thoughtfully. "Well, I wouldn't know about that, Hardy. I'm color-blind, you see."

"Huh?" Beef cried, sitting straight up on the examining table.

"I'm totally color-blind," Dr. Dewlittle admitted with a chuckle. "I've been color-blind my whole life. I can't see colors at all. Good thing I'm a doctor and not a house painter, don't you think?"

Beef fainted, thereby failing the physical exam.

He revived in time to see the four bright blue Space Cadets going into the office for their physical. He saw them greet Dr. Dewlittle and, true to form, Hunk picked up the mouth of the stethoscope and shouted, "Testing one, two, three!" getting quite a reaction from the doctor, who wasn't quick enough in removing it from his ears.

"You fellas are looking in the pink!" Beef heard the doctor say. Then the door closed behind them.

They're going to pass, Beef thought, staggering back to his room. Those four blue baboons are going to pass.

He'd never felt so miserable in all his life.

Commander Dorque had never felt so happy in all his life.

The four Space Cadets had flunked.

They had flunked their written exams. They had flunked their weapons exam. They had even flunked their physical exam.

The doctor couldn't even find a heartbeat on one of those four morons, the one named Andy.

That one was legally dead!

Dorque clapped his hands together in childlike glee and did a little tap dance on top of his desk. He made up a little song, which he sang as he danced, the lyrics consisting of: "They flunked, they flunked, they flunked."

He stopped his dance, suddenly thinking about the other two unfortunate cadets. Hardy and Cheesewell. They had flunked, too.

What a pity.

Two excellent cadets.

Dorque didn't want to see them go. But what choice did he have?

At least they had flunked out of the Academy

and ruined their lives forever for a good cause.

*His* cause.

He would have to send them a letter of thanks to take with them as a farewell present. It was the very least he could do.

"They flunked, they flunked, they flunked." The headmaster resumed his joyful desktop song and dance.

Good-bye to the four Space Cadets. And good-bye to the Space Academy forever.

Hello to a blessed retirement, to a quiet, secluded planet where he could fish all day. And dream of cherry-rhubarb pies.

Only dream of them . . .

Oh, well. Life isn't perfect, he decided.

Not perfectly perfect. But perfect enough!

Commander Dorque was still tap dancing on his desk when the four Space Cadets, Cammy Cheesewell, and Beef Hardy entered to receive their bad news in person. "Oh. Sorry. I was just . . . uh . . . looking for something up here," he told them. He climbed down from the desktop, pulling in his chins, tightening his lips into a hard expression, putting on his most serious face.

All six of them stood in a casual line in front of his desk. The headmaster surveyed them all darkly, his hard expression unchanging.

Am I seeing things, he thought, rubbing his eyes, or are those four clowns bright blue?!

Oh, well. It didn't matter *what* color they were.

Soon he wouldn't have to see their idiotic, grinning faces ever again.

The Commander lowered his voice and began his grim announcement. "I'm sorry to say that I have the most unhappy news for you six cadets," he said softly, his face filled with regret. "The most unhappy news a cadet can receive."

And, then, he just couldn't contain himself. He began giggling, then roaring with laughter. "You flunked, you flunked, you flunked!" he sang, with more joy than he had felt in forty years.

# 15

HAVING RECEIVED THEIR UNHAPPY NEWS, the six cadets had begun trudging silently out of the Commander's office when the door burst open and Debby Dorque rushed in, carrying her camcorder as usual, a determined look on her pretty face.

"Commander Daddy — can I see you for a moment?" she asked.

"Yes, yes," the Commander sang, his eyes twinkling merrily, joy in his heart. "I always have time for you, Debby."

"Well," Debby glanced at the six cadets standing forlornly by the door, "if they could just wait outside. I want to show you something."

"Of course, of course!" her father cried happily.

The cadets obediently trooped out of the office. Debby removed the cassette from the camcorder and strode over to the videotape player on her father's bookshelf.

"What is it you want to show me?" the Commander asked. "Is it something for the class video yearbook, my dear?"

"Perhaps . . ." Debby said mysteriously. "I think you'll find it very interesting, Daddy."

He came over and stood beside her in front of the TV screen. "What is it?" he asked.

"Well, it's a little tape I made from your office closet," Debby said, her expression turning serious. "A little tape of you talking with Cadet Hardy."

"What?" The Commander's face reddened with surprise. "You mean — "

"I have you on tape, Daddy. Plotting with Hardy, telling him to do *anything* to make the four Space Cadets flunk, helping him, conspiring with him."

"Conspiring?" the headmaster choked on the word.

"Yes. Using a cadet to try to hurt four other cadets. It's all on tape," Debby said, patting the cassette.

Commander Dorque rubbed his chins nervously. "And what do you plan to do with this tape, my dear daughter?"

"I plan to show it to the whole school," Debby said. "I want every cadet to see it. There'll be a riot here, Daddy. The cadets will go on strike when they see what kind of leader their headmaster is. They'll all go bananas when they see you tried to rig the exams. Word will get back to your superiors. You'll be in trouble, Daddy. Big trouble."

His daughter was right. Commander Dorque knew the generals. They would use this as an excuse not to give him his pension.

"But, Debby, listen to reason — "

Commander Dorque made a grab for the cassette, but his daughter was too fast for him and held onto it tightly.

"Okay. What's your price?" he asked. He knew when he was beaten.

"Pass Hunk and his three friends," Debby said quickly.

"What?"

"Let Hunk and his friends go on to the next semester," she repeated. "Don't flunk them."

"Don't flunk them?" the Commander asked weakly.

"Let them pass, and I won't show this tape to anyone."

The headmaster swallowed hard. His daughter may not have been great at astronomy or space history, but when it came to blackmail, she was a whiz.

Good officer material, he thought.

"But if I pass those four clowns, that means that only Hardy and Cheesewell flunked out," he said thoughtfully. "That wouldn't be fair. They're my two most loyal cadets."

*Too* loyal, Debby thought.

"I'm sure you can figure something out, Daddy," Debby replied. "You're a very smart man." She tickled him under one of his chins.

"Let me see the tape," he said suddenly.

"What?"

"I *am* a very smart man," he replied. "Show me the tape."

"Okay. Fine." She moved toward the VCR. "I was right there in the closet, Daddy. I've got the whole conversation right here."

She shoved the tape into the machine and pressed the "play" button. The screen was dark for a while, and then filled with a large eyeball.

"What's that? Is that me? You were using a close-up lens?" Commander Dorque asked.

Debby's mouth dropped open in horror.

"I can't hear anything," her father said. "And all I can see is that eyeball."

"Oh, no," Debby said weakly. "I don't believe it." She went pale, looked about to faint. "That's my eyeball. I — I was holding the camcorder backward."

"They flunk!" Commander Dorque cried jubilantly. He started up his happy dance. "They flunk! They flunk! They flunk!"

"I blew it," Debby wailed.

"They flunk! They flunk! They flunk!" The

Commander joyfully took his daughter's hands in his and led her around in an awkward dance.

"Nothing can save them now," he said, grinning so hard his mouth seemed to stretch up to his ears. "Bring them all back in. I want to tell them the bad news one more time!"

# 16

THE SIX CADETS TRUDGED MISERABLY back into the headmaster's office, taking seats in silence across from his enormous, wooden desk. Debby slumped against the far wall, shaking her head unhappily, avoiding Hunk's curious glances.

Commander Dorque stood in front of his desk, his mouth quivering as he tried to suppress a smile. "After further review of your situation," he began, "I'm very sorry to tell you cadets that — "

And then he spotted the object on Hunk's lap.

It was a tin of some sort. A round, silver tin with a silver foil cover.

The headmaster stopped in midsentence and stared at the object held between Hunk's two hands. He sniffed the air.

"Hunk," he said, eyes on the tin, "may I ask what is that object in your lap?"

"This?" Hunk held it up. "It's a pie tin, sir."

No one else looked up at it. Everyone was too depressed and miserable.

"And, if I may ask, what is *in* the pie tin?" Dorque asked, his eyes bulging in his head.

"A pie, sir," Hunk replied, lowering the tin back to his lap.

"And if I may further inquire," said the Commander, leaning forward as if to hear the answer sooner, "what kind of pie does the tin contain?"

"It's a cherry-rhubarb pie, sir," Hunk told him.

None of the other failed cadets looked up or made a sound. If they had looked up, they would have seen the Commander's tongue flop out, and they would have seen him begin to drool on the carpet like a dog.

"My aunt just gave it to me, Commander Dorque," Hunk said, tapping the pie tin with his fingers.

"Your aunt?"

"Yeah. Aunt Carmella. She kinda looks after me, you know. Tries to fatten me up. She's always giving me cherry-rhubarb pies. I don't even like them that much."

Dorque's eyes had completely glazed over. He hadn't heard a word Hunk had said.

Across the room, Debby stood up straight and perked up her ears. She had the distinct feeling something important was happening here.

"Carmella Flan is your aunt?" her father asked Hunk.

"Yes, sir. Aunt Carmella helped me get into the Academy," Hunk said.

"And she gives you pies?"

"Yes. At least two or three a week. I really don't know what to do with them all."

"She gives you pies?"

"You already asked me that question, sir," Hunk said.

"Oh. Did I?" The Commander reached out a hand and rolled his tongue back into his mouth. "Hunk, could I see you in private? I'd like to discuss . . . uh . . . your situation with you."

"Okay, sir," Hunk said, standing up, a confused look on his face.

"And . . . uh . . . bring the pie tin with you, okay?"

"Okay." Hunk began to follow the headmaster back to his inner chamber behind the front office.

"The rest of you are dismissed," Commander Dorque said, gesturing for everyone else to leave. With trembling hands, he reached out and took the pie tin from Hunk. "Let me help you carry that — *son*." And they disppeared into the tiny back room.

A few hours later, the four Space Cadets were changing their uniforms, getting ready to go down to the rec room and celebrate their good news.

"Why do you think the Commander changed

his mind and passed us?" Shaky asked.

"I don't know," Hunk said, scratching his head. "After I gave him the pie and agreed to give him two or three more every week, his whole attitude changed. I guess he just finally realized how valuable we are to the Academy."

"I think maybe he added up the test scores again and saw that we actually passed," Rip said.

"I don't see why I failed the physical, just because I don't have a heart," Andy griped. "I have a twelve-valve compressor which is much more efficient."

"Well, anyway — we passed!" Hunk declared happily. "We're all gonna be Space Patrolmen. We're gonna be heroes. Just like in the comic books."

"The Commander passed Cheesewell and Hardy, too," Shaky informed them. "He said he was declaring it 'National Everyone Passes This Semester Week.'"

"Yo! Let's go celebrate!" Hunk cried.

"Ha . . . ha . . . ho . . . hee . . ." Andy added, for no reason at all.

"Hey — I need a sock," Rip said, bending down and searching the floor beneath his bunk.

"What did you say?" Hunk asked, grinning.

"I need a sock."

Hunk socked Rip. Andy socked Hunk. Rip socked Andy. Shaky socked himself.

They were happily socking each other when

the door burst open and in walked Debby Dorque.

"Hunk — what are you doing?" she exclaimed.

"Uh . . . studying?" he replied.

"But exams are over. Everyone has passed," she said.

"Yeah. Isn't it great? I guess your dad decided he just couldn't live without us."

"I guess," Debby said, unable to suppress a smile. "Come on, Hunk," she said softly. "Why don't you and I go for a long, romantic walk in the moonlight?"

"I'll go for that," Hunk said, giving her his most winning smile.

"Me, too!" Rip called.

"Count me in!" called Shaky.

"Beep. Nine forty-five. Me, too!" said Andy.

And the five of them headed out arm-in-arm toward the Academy gardens.

Look out, Universe! The Space Cadets are about to blast off for their first interplanetary mission!

Watch for Book Two: *Losers in Space*.

## About the Author

R.L. STINE is the author of more than one hundred books of humor, adventure, horror, and mystery for young readers. In addition to his publishing work, he is head writer of the children's TV show *Eureeka's Castle*. *Jerks-in-Training* is the first of his series SPACE CADETS.

Mr. Stine lives in New York City with his wife, Jane, and their son, Matt.

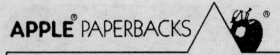

## by Ann M. Martin